Love and Death in
BEIJING

A Love and Death &
Political Espionage Novel

Volume 4

Hal Graff

Copyright © 2023 **Harold Graff II Publishing**

All rights reserved. No part of this publication may be reproduced, distributed, or transmitted in any form or by any means, including photocopying, recording, or other electronic or mechanical methods, without the prior written permission of the publisher, except in the case of brief quotations embodied in critical reviews and certain other noncommercial uses permitted by copyright law. For permission requests, write to the publisher, addressed "Attention: Book Rights and Permission," at the address below.

Published in the United States of America

ISBN 978-1-961507-57-9 (SC)
ISBN 978-1-961507-55-5 (HC)
ISBN 978-1-961507-56-2 (Ebook)

Harold Graff II Publishing
222 West 6th Street
Suite 400, San Pedro, CA, 90731
sec26para5@yahoo.com

Ordering Information and Rights Permission:

Quantity sales. Special discounts might be available on quantity purchases by corporations, associations, and others. For details, contact the publisher at the address above.

For Book Rights Adaptation and other Rights Permission. Call us at toll-free 1-888-945-8513 or send us an email at admin@stellarliterary.com.

For Eric, Lainen, Colton, Ethan, Jenny, Scott, Finn, and Kade

And for my Creator, my God in Heaven, my Lord and Savior, Jesus Christ, my comforter, and guide, the Holy Spirit, and the Holy Trinity

NOVELS BY DR. HAL GRAFF
(6,478,043 total published words)

The Love and Death Series
Harold Gatewood Mysteries
(Mystery / Political Espionage)

Love and Death at the Encierro Vol. 1
Love and Death in Cuba Vol. 2
Love and Death in Tokyo Vol. 3
Love and Death in Beijing Vol. 4
Love and Death in London Vol. 5
Love and Death in Korea Vol. 6
Love and Death in Venezuela Vol. 7
Love and Death in Mexico Vol. 8
Love and Death in the Dominican Republic Vol. 9
Love and Death: a Journey Vol. 10
Love and Death in Tuscon Vol. 11
The Harold Gatewood Mysteries: An Encyclopedia Vol. 12 (For my use only)
Love and Death in Virginia Vol. 13
Love and Death in Chile Vol. 14
Love and Death in Paris Vol.15
Love and Death in the Orient Vol. 16
Love and Death in the China Sea Vol. 17
Love and Death in Caracas Vol. 18
Love and Death in Chicago Vol. 19
Love and Death in Moscow Vol. 20
Love and Death in the Ukraine Vol. 21
Love and Death in Rome Vol. 22
The Harold Gatewood Mysteries: An Encyclopedia Vol. 2 (Vol. 2 is for my use only)
Love and Death in the British Isles Vol. 24
Love and Death in the Philippines Vol. 25
Love and Death in Barcelona Vol. 26
Gatewood Returns Vol. 27

The Davis Finn Mysteries
(Historical Fiction / Mystery / Political Espionage)

Murder in Georgia Vol. 1 (A Quadrilogy – Book 1)
Murder in Montana Vol. 2 (A Quadrilogy - Book 2)
Murder in the FBI Vol. 3 (A Quadrilogy – Book 3)
Murder in Vietnam Vol. 4 (A Quadrilogy – Book 4)
Angel of Mercy Vol. 5
Oxy Vol. 6 (A Trilogy – Book 1)
The White Duck Vol. 7 (A Trilogy – Book 2)
Sucker Punch Vol. 8 (A Trilogy – Book 3)
Eddy Vol. 9
Counterfeit Vol. 10 (A Trilogy – Book 1)
Montenegro Vol. 11 (A Trilogy – Book 2)
Triple Crown Vol. 12 (A Trilogy – Book 3)
Murder in Oxford Vol. 13 (A Trilogy – Book 1)
Revenge Vol. 14 (A Trilogy – Book 2)
Survival Vol. 15 (A Trilogy – Book 3)
The Mississippi Hangman Vol. 16 (A Trilogy – Book 1)
A Dead President Vol. 17 (A Trilogy – Book 2)
Oath of Office Vol. 18 (A Trilogy – Book 3)
Finn and Gatewood's Outdoor Adventures Vol. 19
Stockholm Syndrome Vol. 20 (A Trilogy – Book 1)
Blood Feud Vol. 21 (A Trilogy – Book 2)
A Terrible Tragedy Vol. 22 (A Trilogy – Book 3)
Takedown Vol.23
Blackmail Vol. 24
Dead Like Lincoln Vol. 25
Lethal Force Vol. 26
The Leopard Vol. 27
The Crossbow Killer Vol. 28
The Ten Pin Killer Vol. 29
The Grand Bargain Vol. 30
Jill Vol. 31 (A Trilogy – Book 1)
Double-cross Vol. 32 (A Trilogy – Book 2)
The Seven Iron Murders Vol.33 (A Trilogy – Book 3)
The Corner Pocket Killer Vol. 34

The Choke Hold Murders Vol. 36
The Midterm Elections Vol. 37
Death Dressed in Blue Vol. 38
His Better Half Vol. 39
Ten Little Indians Vol. 40 (A Trilogy – Book 1)
The Cassowary Vol. 41 (A Trilogy – Book 2)
Remember, Remember, the 5th Of November Vol. 42 (A Trilogy – Book 3)

The Parker Weston Romance, Action, Mysteries

Penelope Vol. 1 (A Trilogy – Book 1)
The Bad Boy Vol. 2 (A Trilogy – Book 2)
Tall Buffalo Vol. 3 (A Trilogy – Book 3)
1, 2, 3, 4, Enter Murder's Door Vol. 4 (A Trilogy – Book 1)
The Sky's the Limit, John Vol. 5 (A Trilogy – Book 2)
Love Will Keep Us Together Vol. 6 (A Trilogy – Book 3)

The Bobby Ross Faith Series

Bobby Ross and the White Stones Vol. 1

The Aidan Conall Mysteries

Carnage at Harvard Vol. 1 (A Trilogy – Book 1)
Its Forty – Love Vol. 2 (A Trilogy – Book 2)
Its Match Point Vol. 3 (A Trilogy – Book 3)

Table of Contents

Author's Note ix
Prologue x
Chapter 1 "Away we go." 1
Chapter 2 "This is Akemi" 4
Chapter 3 "Hi Pat" 10
Chapter 4 "I don't believe it" 15
Chapter 5 "Come in Harold" 20
Chapter 6 To the Tokyo Dome 27
Chapter 7 Meet The Parents 34
Chapter 8 "Of course, I do." 43
Chapter 9 "What are my options?" 50
Chapter 10 Good News for the New Year 57
Chapter 11 Settling Old Scores 62
Chapter 12 "This Time" 68
Chapter 13 Retirement 74
Chapter 14 Getting Ready 82
Chapter 15 "How was your day?" 87
Chapter 16 "By plane" 93
Chapter 17 "I am Ready" 98
Chapter 18 Three Month Review 103
Chapter 19 "Like a clock?" 108
Chapter 20 The Succession 116
Chapter 21 "I am Here" 120
Chapter 22 Check the dates 125
Chapter 23 A Tangled Web 132
Chapter 24 "We want to talk with you" 137
Chapter 25 "What's that?" 141

Chapter 26 Purgatory 146
Chapter 27 The Tiger Lives 153
Chapter 28 Boomerang 160
Chapter 29 Innocent 165
Chapter 30 "Mission Accomplished" 169
Chapter 31 Taimen 175

Author's Note

Welcome, to "Love and Death in Beijing", the fourth novel in the "Love and Death" series, featuring the main character, Harold Gatewood.

As with all the novels I write, it is my honor, privilege, and my pleasure, to bring you this thrilling political espionage, mystery, novel.

I know you're going to love it.

Blessings,

Dr. Hal Graff

Prologue

October 28

"LET'S MAKE IT OFFICIAL"
"I love you honey. It is time that I ask your father to grant me permission to marry you."

Akemi enthusiastically agreed, stating the she was excited about the couple starting their new life together on an official basis, and that their parents would be thrilled with the news.

She had been looking forward to taking the trip to Illinois to meet Harold's parents, and then taking her husband to be to Beijing to meet her parents, and get her father and mother's blessing on the marriage.

Akemi had accelerated her Masters classes and was finished with the course work, and comprehensive exams. Her thesis was done except for minor touch up work which she would finish during the time she was in America and China.

She could then be a fulltime wife for Harold, in Tokyo, or wherever their lives would take them.

They would fly to America the next day, as Harold had surprised her with their tickets, and one for her bodyguard, Yong Wei.

Her loyal protector had saved her life, and would hopefully not be needed, but should be with them, as the danger from the Yakuza crime family, and the ever-present AIO terrorist group, might still be present.

In any case, it would be a wonderful time in Harold and Akemi's lives, and she looked forward to meeting her new in-laws and presenting her true love to her parents.

Chapter 1

"Away we go."

October 29

AKEMI HAD DECLARED herself ready for the trip, and had closed the lid on her suitcase even before Harold had started to pack.

With some prodding, she admitted that her suitcase had been packed for two days before Harold had told her they would be leaving, as she had seen the tickets, he had left on the bedroom chest of drawers.

Harold loved the fact that she was observant, and was usually on pace, and often ahead of him, in all matters.

Harold's packing was also quick, as he had clothes in his home in Central Illinois, and would only need a skeleton list of items.

Yong Wei also traveled light, with dark clothes, personal items, and his Chinese stars, which had been used to dispatch Kimiko during her assault on Akemi.

They would travel light, as there were laundry facilities in his house.

The plan was to spend two weeks in Illinois, as Harold wanted Akemi to meet his parents, and needed to discuss some business matters with his parents and his lawyer.

They would then return to Tokyo for a week when Harold would discuss his contract offer from the Tokyo Cardinals, then head to Beijing for two weeks to meet her parents and get permission to marry Akemi.

The flight was an easy one, with no safety episodes. Despite its length, it gave everyone a chance to relax.

Akemi worked on her thesis, and listened to the inflight entertainment.

She was intrigued by watching the lost episodes of "The Honeymooners", starring Jackie Gleason, laughing at the main character's funny dancing skills, and his statement of "Away we go".

Akemi also told Harold that is what they had done when they left on the plane that morning. A few hours into the trip she fell asleep, resting her head on Harold's shoulder.

While she was napping, Harold thought about how the trip had reminded him of several of the events of the last three years which had impacted his life.

He thought back to the initial trip to Spain when he had first become ostracized from baseball.

Harold remembered meeting Lore Lehoi, falling in love with her, meeting her parents, helping solve the San Toro de Lidia murder spree killings, dealing with the killer Zigor Kerbasi.

He had also helped the Agence de Renseignement, and the local police department, prevent the AIO terrorist organization plot Operation Ice Chest, which was designed to blow up the Plaza de Toros Bulling Stadium in Pamplona, a national symbol.

Gatewood painfully recalled how Zigor and Lore had both tried to kill him, and the attack by Resignment Lore's jilted ex-fiancé and bullfighter Andoni Mikola.

Both times his life had been saved by San Toro de Lidia Homicide Detectives Jakome and Iker.

Other memories flooded his mind. He remembered the year after the initial trip to the festival, when he was asked back by the King of Spain to receive the Order of Civil Merit for his contributions in preventing the AIO's plot.

A few months later, he had returned to Spain to be honored by the city of San Toro de Lidia by officially opening the festival of San Fermin and the Running of The Bulls.

He then recalled how he had left Spain for Cuba, to scout the World Baseball Games for Major League baseball, and how he had met and fallen in love with the beautiful Christina Abene, the secretary for the President of Cuba, Alberto Bertalina.

He shuddered as he remembered how he had become embroiled in the coup attempt to overthrow the Cuban government, had helped save the President's life, had survived assassination attempts on his life by AIO assassin Bakar Kemen at Jucaro and Pinar Del Rio.

Harold had also endured Christina dying in his arms at the airport the day they were to leave, a victim of the Kamen's gunfire.

He also thought about the events of the next chapter of his life, going to Tokyo to continue his baseball comeback with the Giants, dealing with the mentally challenged female Yakuza crime princess Kimiko Hayato.

He also survived AIO hitman Bittor Kemen's attacks. Harold had also almost seen Akemi being killed a few days before they had left on the trip back to America.

Harold had also faced the possible end of his baseball playing days at the highest level in the world, the pain from the multiple surgeries on his arm and shoulder, and the uncertainty if he would ever regain his dream of returning to the big leagues.

The totality of what had taken place in the last three years had taken a toll on him.

But, as he looked at Akemi napping next to him, he knew it had all been worth the pain, torment, dismay, danger, and depression to get to this point.

Harold was tired, but wonderfully, totally, happy. He wanted to see his parents, and then settle into his new life, whatever that would bring, with the beautiful Asian woman next to him.

Chapter 2

"This is Akemi"

October 29

IT WAS EVENING when the commuter flight from Chicago O'Hare airport landed in Bloomington, Illinois.

Harold saw his parents waving and smiling as he and Akemi walked toward the receiving area beyond the security and entry area.

He pointed out his parents to Akemi, and they both smiled and waved in return.

After they had all hugged and said hello, Harold smiled and said, "This is Akemi".

Harold also introduced Akemi's bodyguard, Yong Wei. Harold had covered the reason why Yong was with them on the trip, saying that he was assigned the task of protecting Akemi, as her father was a man of great importance in China.

Everyone was relaxed and enjoying themselves, asking and talking about the two flights which had brought the couple to Bloomington.

The conversation continued at the baggage claim area, on the walk to the car in short term parking in front of the airport, and on the thirty-minute ride to Harold's hometown, Gibson City, Illinois.

The ride was a short, yet an enjoyable one. Yong Wei took up half of the back seat due to his size, forcing Akemi to sit on Harold's lap, which was fine for both of them.

They stopped at Harold's parents' house, ate, and relaxed until it was time to retire for the evening.

Harold and Akemi would stay in his house, less than a mile from his parents' home on the outskirts of town. Young Wei would stay in the guest room in Harold's home.

His home had always been his refuge from the outside world, a place of peace where he could surround himself with the things most important to him, his books, his hobbies, his thoughts, and his family.

His home was a beautiful brick ranch with a massive cathedral ceiling living room at the rear of the home, a large foyer, five bedrooms, three baths, a large den which also served as his office, a dining room, a large kitchen area, a workshop, and a four-car garage.

On the walls of the living room were the Harold's hunting and fishing trophies including a wild boar shot in Tennessee, and a pheasant shot in Illinois.

Also present were a swan taken in North Carolina, a Canadian goose killed in Illinois, a kudu, a gemsbok, a blesbok, a steenbuck, and three springbucks, a white, black, and common brown colored all from South Africa, and a large Northern Pike fish caught in Ontario, Canada.

Akemi was amazed and looked at the taxidermy mounts for several minute sold about each of the animals and what it was like to have had the experience of taking them, and the details of each trip.

Harold was glad she liked the outdoors, and planned to take her on many nice trips.

A full finished basement was stocked with a pool table, ping pong table, a collection of big screen tv's, and a theatre room for watching movies and tapes his father had compiled of Harold's hitting and fielding mechanics over his nine-year career.

The garage was home to his luxury car, and his full-size pickup truck.

He was not a car guy, but his one antique car, bought for investment purposes and as a reminder of the first car he had legally driven, a 1959 four door hardtop Plymouth Belvidere, with push button drive on the dashboard and high tailfins at the back of the vehicle.

The vintage car had always had created a special memory of an enjoyable period in his life, was at home in the spacious garage.

Behind the house was a matching red brick, with rough white rough finish, building stocked with a pitching machine, netted hitting cage, various models of batting tees and hitting aides, and workout machines.

There was also an office with baseball related training materials, and results of his Doctoral dissertation on the motivation factors which impacted performance results of major league baseball players.

The home was set on a hill, on five acres, just North of his hometown, and his parent's home. Large hardwood trees formed perfect additions to the view of the home from the road.

The property behind the home, eighty acres of farmland, was also owned by Gatewood, and provided an area where he could hunt the few remaining pheasants in Illinois in November and December, even though the hunting had deteriorated to that of taking a nice walk.

After the guided tour of his home, Harold asked Akemi if she was tired, and ready for bed.

They retired for the night, made love for the first time in America, and then settled in for a long sleep, awaking at ten the next morning.

Refreshed, and having conquered jet lag, the couple was ready for breakfast.

Harold doubted there was anything in the refrigerator or cupboards, but was surprised to see both were full, as his mother had made sure they would not go hungry, after making a stop at the grocery store.

The next two weeks would encompass relaxing, having Akemi get to know parents, and Harold taking care of needed business on the farms, his investments, and his baseball related contract duties with his lawyer and agent.

The day after their arrival was spent visiting with his parents. It was a mutual benefit association type of meeting as Akemi loved his parents and they loved her.

Harold and his dad covered the farm business while Akemi helped his mom, and finished some items on her Masers thesis.

After lunch, Harold's dad called he, Akemi, and his mom into his parents' den, as he wanted to show them something.

"I want you all to see the results of Harold and my fishing trip to Canada last year."

Harold smiled and Akemi's eyes widened at the sight of three large mounted fish on the den walls.

"Dad, your mounts are back already."

"Yes. Let me show them to you."

"Okay."

"Akemi, this is my trophy smallmouth bass."

"It is beautiful. How big is it?"

"Six pounds, and two ounces."

"What did you use to catch it?"

"Harold made me a French spinner. It did the trick."

"That is a beautiful fish."

"Yes, it is. I love the beautiful brown coloration. Do you have bass in China?"

"Yes. We have both types, largemouth and smallmouth."

"Wonderful."

"What is that fish, the one with big eyes?"

"It is a walleye Akemi."

"It is big. What did it weigh?"

"Eleven pounds."

"Oh, my."

"Do you have walleye in China?"

"No. I have never seen one before."
"This one is a very nice sized trophy."
"What did you use to catch it?"
"We were trolling when I hooked that one. I was using a walleye spinner, colored orange, with a minnow attached."
"What is that one?"
"It is a musky."
"It is huge! How big was it?"
"Sixty pounds, and one ounce."
"It is a monster."
'It was fifty=eight inches long."
"How long did it take to reel him in to the boat?"
"Twenty-five minutes."
"Were your arms tired?"
"Yes."
"How did you get it in the boat/"
"Harold used a fish cradle."
"What is that?"
"It is a net with a board on each end. It is used to calm the fish when it is near the boat and ready to be brought on board"
"How does it work?"
"The fish is led into the bet, which is below the fish. The net is then raised with the fish in it, and lifted on board."
"Did it work?"
"It was great until the fish slipped out of the net in the boat."
"Then what happened?"
"It thrashed around the bottom of the boat, knocking over tackle boxes, pop cans, and other things, until Harold reached down and picked it up."
"What did he do then?"
"He used a long hook remover to take the lure out of the fish's mouth."
"It is beautiful. And, it has long teeth."
"Yes, they can be dangerous."
"What kind of lure is that?"
"It is a suick."
"A what?"
"A suick, Akemi."
"How does it work?"
"You heave it out on to the top of the water, and work it back to the boat in about one-foot pulls."
"Did Harold catch any fish?"

"He didn't catch many big smallmouth bass or walleye, but he caught a very big Northern Pike."

Harold then asked his dad a question. "Did my fish get mounted yet?"

"It is funny you asked that. I have it in the walk-in closet in the bedroom. Let's take a look at it."

"It looks great, Dad."

"When you know where you want to put it in the house let me know an I will help you put it up."

"Dad, and mom, did you know that Akemi is also a good fisherperson?"

"Good for her."

"We caught quite a few nice Chum and Pink salmon a couple weeks ago in Japan."

"That's great. She will have lots of fun doing that with you."

"Yes, she says she likes it even more than basketball. Dad, we will soon have another good fisherperson in the family. We are getting married."

"Oh, that is wonderful. Congratulations, Akemi."

"Thank you."

"Harold's mother said "Welcome to the family Akemi."

"Thank you so much."

"Your Mom and I think that you both made a great catch."

After many hugs and handshakes, the couple was able to sit down and relax, and talk for a few minutes before heading back to Harold's home.

Once there they settled down onto the couch, and Harold asked her a question.

"Did that announcement surprise you,"

"A little, Harold."

"It seemed like a perfect time. And, I didn't want to wait.

I wanted them to know how much I love you, and that we wanted to be together."

"Thank you. I am so happy we told then right away."

"Me too. I couldn't keep the secret much longer."

"Me either."

"I don't think that they were that surprised, based on my phone calls and letters."

"What did you tell them about me."

"I told them what a wonderful woman you are, and that I cared for you very much."

"That was so sweet."

"And, I told them that we are perfectly matched for each other."

"Yes, that is what I have also told my parents."

"Akemi, the American part of that mission is completed. Let's go celebrate."

"Where are we going?"

"Right there, Honey."

With that comment Harold led Akemi to the master bedroom, where they made love to christen their engagement announcement.

Chapter 3

"Hi Pat"

October 30

TODAY, HAROLD NEEDED to go to see his lawyer in Bloomington and set up the legal requirements Akemi and he had agreed to before they left Japan.

They each would keep separate estates and start the clock ticking once they were married.

Each of their property prior to their marriage would remain as it were before they were married, and each had agreed not to touch the inheritances each would receive from their respective parents.

Both would receive about the same amount of property from their families, as all people involved had become successful in their own right.

Once they would have children, they would set up trusts and address what property they had accumulated together.

Harold and Akemi both liked the sound of the phrase "once they would have children", and looked forward to that day, whenever it might arrive.

They both wanted to wait a bit before children arrived. They wanted two children, as Akemi wanted to break the one child rule of China, as she had missed having a sibling.

Harold had teased her and said they needed two so that they could play catch with each other when he was not around.

When the legal appointment was over, Harold wanted to go past the ballpark of the Central Illinois Magicians and talk to the people who still worked there, and to see his manager from a few months ago, Pat Sullivan.

He was able to speak with the people in the office, the general manager, and the groundskeeper. It was great to see them, as he had appreciated his time with the Magicians, who had treated him nicely, and had given him an opportunity to play ball when no one else would.

Pat Sullivan was in his office in a conference with a newly signed player for next season. When they were through, they walked into the clubhouse where Harold was waiting for them.

"Harold. It is great to see you."

"Thanks Pat. It is great to see you too."

"How are you?"

"I am doing great Pat. How are you?"

"I am fine. Things here have been good."

"That's wonderful Pat. You were developing some nice young players when I was with you earlier this year."

"Harold, this is Thomas Jares. He is a left-handed pitcher who was with the Orioles organization two years ago."

"It is nice to meet you, Thomas. Who was the scout who signed you?"

"Zack Wilson."

"He is a good man."

"How do you know him?"

"We were teammates in the minor leagues."

"Harold, I played one year in the Orioles system, and then suffered an arm injury."

"Did you have surgery "

"Yes."

"Who did it?"

"Doctor Doug Robinson."

"He is the best. He did mine a couple years ago."

"Did your arm come back?"

"Yes, almost one hundred percent, so far."

"That is good to hear."

"You will in fine. The success rate is very high."

"What position did you play Harold?"

"I caught for nine years. Now I am in left field, and I can play third and first base."

Pat Sullivan took his turn to speak, as he wanted to give encouragement to Thomas Jares.

"Thomas, the man you are speaking with was the best catcher in the major leagues for nine years.

He was with us at the beginning of the year last year, until we sold his contract to the Tokyo Giants."

"He must have been a good player for you."

"He is the best. He knows baseball, always hustles, and plays hard every day."

"That is the type of player I like to have as a teammate."

"He came here, did everything we asked, made the All-Star team, and then went to Japan. He then played great there. I think he will be back in the majors very soon."

"I wish you the best Mr. Gatewood."

"Thank you. I wish you well Thomas. Do your best. Pat is a great developer of young players, knows how the game is played, and will help you in your career. Do everything he asks."

"I will. It was nice to meet you, Mr. Gatewood."

After the young pitcher had left, Harold and Pat had a chance to visit.

"How does it look for the coming year, Pat?"

"Pretty good. We have picked up some good players, along with a few of the guys who were here when you here with us. We should be pretty good."

"I wanted to thank you, Pat."

"For what Harold"

For giving me a chance when I was down, and almost out."

"You were never at that point, Harold. You only thought you were at that time. You have a lot left yet, Harold. You can be back in the majors soon."

"Thanks. I think I can."

"I read where you were playing great in Japan."

"Thanks. I am almost back, Pat."

"Several people have asked me about you and I always tell them to get off their duff and sign you, before you are signed by someone else."

"I appreciate that, Pat."

"Do you have any offers, Harold?"

"No. My agent gets some inquires, but nothing yet."

"Let me know if I can ever do anything for you. What are you going to do Harold?"

"I am here for a couple weeks, then I will go back to Tokyo. They were very pleased with my work this season. I fit right into their system."

"How did you like Japanese baseball?"

"It wasn't the majors. That being said, I loved it there."

"Yes, I have heard that it is quite an experience."

"Oh yes. Balloons, cheering sections, formalities, all of which I loved. If I don't get signed with a big-league club I would love to go back there."

"You know you are always welcome here, Harold."

"Thanks, Pat. I really appreciate all that you have done for me."

"Harold, how is it going personally? I know you have been through hell, and high water, the last couple years."

"It has been tough. This year was another unbelievable experience in Tokyo."

"I heard some rumors. What happened?"

"Pat, I have never seen anything like it. I go to play ball and without really doing anything, terrorists are trying to kill me, beautiful but lunatic women are making my life miserable, and I am somehow involved in international political situations."

"What happened this time?'

"I dated a beautiful girl who ended up being involved with the Yakuza, the crime mob in Tokyo. She stalked me, and almost ended up killing my fiancé."

"What else happened?"

"The AIO terrorist organization tried to kill me again."

"Was it related to the actions you took in Spain to stop their plan?"

"Yes. They never give up."

"Maybe you should stay here in the United States and try to hook on with a team. It might be safer."

"I have thought about it."

"Did you say you were engaged?"

"Yes."

"Congratulations."

"Thanks, Pat."

"Let me guess, Harold. She is beautiful, intelligent, and a great person."

"You're right on all of those counts, Pat.'

"I am sure she is quite wonderful, Harold. I wish the best for both of you."

"Thanks Pat. She is quite a woman."

"You deserve happiness, Harold."

"Pat, I want to ask you something."

"Sure, go ahead."

"Why aren't you managing or coaching in the major Leagues? You are as good a manager as there is, and certainly as good as anyone I have ever had the honor of playing for."

"Thanks, Harold. I get some offers but none that fit in with what I see as my path to the big leagues."

"I think you would get some great offers very soon."

"Thanks, Harold."

"If I can put a good word in for you, please let me know."

"Thanks, Harold."

"Well, I should head home to Gibson City. It was great to see you."

"Come back again."

"I will."

On the way home Harold thought about their conversation. "Pat should be managing or coaching in the big leagues. Maybe he would get his shot."

Harold also wondered about Pat's comment about maybe staying in the United States, to avoid being chased by terrorists and assassins again.

He let the thought pass, and drove the same road, route nine, he had driven for years, to his college, his years playing in the Central Illinois Collegiate League, and his stint with the Magicians.

The difference now was that he was going home to be with a woman he truly loved, Akemi.

Chapter 4

"I don't believe it"

October 31

HAROLD WATCHED AKEMI s she slept.

She was truly beautiful, with her mid-back length dark black hair, perfectly, shaped, Fibonacci, beautiful face, dark brown eyes, and perfect, hour-glass, shaped body.

He had been with many other beautiful women, with Lore Lehoi and Christina Abene heading the list, but Akemi was the only woman who had totally captured his interest, and his heart.

She opened her eyes, smiled at him, and asked what they were going to do today.

Harold replied that they were going to have a busy day, since it was a beautiful, Indian Summer Halloween Day.

The second item on the agenda was a trip to the golf course with his parents would indoctrinate Akemi to the game, after which they would eat supper at the nineteen holes, then return to a Halloween party, with twenty of his high school classmates in attendance.

Akemi said that the day sounded wonderful but wondered what the first item of the day was to be.

Harold leaned over kissed here, and said "This".

He then proceeded to make love with her. When they had finished, they exchanged "I love you" pledges, and showered together in anticipation of the day's events.

Everyone had been enjoying the couple's visit.

Harold's parents were thrilled with the news of the engagement, and the many people in town who had stopped by to say hello had told the couple how wonderful it was that they had found each other and had wished them well.

Yong Wei had been enjoying his relaxed, laid-back, protection assignment, and his daily workouts in the training building.

Harold and Akemi were relishing their daily workouts in the exercise building, the relaxed small-town atmosphere, and their time together.

Due to Yong Wei's body size, the couple had to take two cars to the golf course.

Harold's parents had a golf cart at the course, but a second one was needed to accommodate the group of five.

Harold would drive one cart, but not play, as he didn't want to risk injury to his shoulder. Akemi would ride with him, with Harold's parents in the second cart.

The golfers would change carts as the locations of their shots during the round would dictate.

Yong Wei would walk, as his size would challenge the strength of the cart.

Harold told Akemi that they were playing for fun, to enjoy it, and not to worry about the results of the round.

She was always a good sport, and was athletic enough to catch on to the mechanics of the gold swing after a few minutes on the practice tee and putting green.

She took to the game immediately, and was enjoying the outing, the fresh air, and the company.

As the round progressed, everyone had an opportunity to talk. Harold and his dad talked about the farms, their South Dakota pheasant hunting trip the year before, upcoming fishing plans, and Harold's upcoming baseball plans.

Harold's mother and Akemi were able to talk about how Akemi and Harold had met.

"We are so glad that you came to visit us Akemi."

"Thank you for asking me."

"You two are a good match."

"Yes, we get along wonderfully."

"I can tell that Harold loves you very much."

"How?"

"Because he looks at you very differently than he has at any woman before you. He is very much in love with you."

"I love him very much."

"I know you do. He is very perceptive on what is best, for both of you."

"I know. I felt that when we were first getting to know each other."

"He will always treat you like the beautiful lady that you are, and he will make sure that you will always be happy."

"He has always been so nice, and charming, from the first time we met."

"When did you two meet?"

"We lived in the same apartment building."

"Did you meet as soon as he arrived in Tokyo?"

"I have to laugh because he did not know that we lived across the hall from each other until a few weeks had passed."

"How did you manage that?"

"I saw him move in, and thought he was handsome. I confess that I would watch him through the door peep hole when he would enter and leave his apartment. I hope that does not upset you."

"No, of course not. I think it is cute. He had no idea that you were checking him out?"

"No."

"How did things progress from there?"

"The newspaper had a big article on his signing with Giants. When I read it, I realized what type of man he might be."

"What happened then"

"I realized what he had been through the years before he arrived in Tokyo, and knew he was a man of character."

"Yes, he is that."

"Each morning, I would do my Tai chi workouts in the courtyard in front of the apartment building.

When would leave to walk to the ballpark, he would stop, bow to me, smile his boyish smile at me, then leave. I looked forward to seeing him every morning, and found him interesting, and accomplished."

"Did he continue that every day?"

"Yes. He was so respectful of my culture, and of me."

"He is a very considerate man."

"He was so cute. I did not smile at him for quite a few mornings in the courtyard. When I knew I wanted to meet him, I smiled."

"You were playing hard to get. Good for you."

"Not really. I was still deciding what kind of man he was."

"When did he first speak to you?"

"He handed me his business card, and a note in English and Chinese, that asked me to contact my father for the permission to take me on a date to become acquainted with each other."

"Oh, how nice. What did you tell your father?"

I told him that Harold was an honorable man of high character, was thoughtful, lived a clean life, and was a man like my father. And, I told him that they both would approve of him."

'They gave you their blessings to meet him."

"Yes. From the first time we were together we were on the same wavelength, and had fun. We like being with each other."

"That is wonderful. If a couple has that they can deal with the ups and downs of life, and be happy together."

"Yes, this has been the happiest time of my life."

"When did he propose to you?"

"After the woman from the Yakuza crime family, Kimiko Hayato, tried to kill me. Yong Wei saved my life by killing her before she got the job done.

When that happened Harold ran to my side, and held me in his arms, and asked me to marry him in the Japanese language, and I said yes."

'We are so glad that you were not hurt Akemi. And, we are so happy that you said yes. You are both made for each other. Harold, and you, could not have made better choices."

"Thank you so much. I was naturally nervous about meeting you. You and your husband are so much like my parents.'

"We love you and am glad you are going to be our daughter, the one I never had."

"Thank you. I was so worried that you would not like the fact that my parents are Japanese, on my mother's side of the family, and Chinese, on my father's side."

"We like people for what they are, not for what they have, or where they live, or what they do for a living. We are thrilled to have you in the family, and know that your parents are wonderful people to have raised such a nice daughter as you."

"Thank you so much. I want you all to come to the wedding."

"We would not miss it, Akemi."

"Thank you."

The group would only play nine holes of golf today as the

Halloween festivities would require Harold and Akemi to meet friends early in the evening.

The group headed into the seventh hole, a short one hundred forty yards from the women's tee, where the women would tee off. Harold's mom had the honors and lofted a high, towering eight iron shot towards the green, which came to rest ten feet from the pin.

Akemi was next, and selected a seven iron for her approach shot. She rolled her hips and body through the swing, followed through toward the green, and watched as her ball hit short of the apron of the green, rolled onward toward the flag, and curved to the right in line with the cup, then softly dropped in for a hole-in-one.

Everyone, including Yong Wei, was stunned, as the shot had been a beautiful, perfect shot.

Harold's comments broke the silence, "I don't believe it!" "Nice shot!"

Akemi didn't realize her accomplishment, and was unsure why everyone was shaking her hand, hugging her, and congratulating her on her shot. A hole-in-one on her first round of golf was an almost unheard-of event.

She had joined the Gatewood hole-in-one club, as Harold's Dad had shot three in his many years of golfing, his mother had one, and even Harold had one, even thought he had rarely played golf as he did not want it to interfere with his baseball skills.

The rest of the round, and the evening, meeting his high school friends from Gibson City, all loyal Greyhound fans, was also enjoyable.

When the couple went to bed that evening, after making love, Akemi told Harold that she loved his father and mother because they reminded her of her own family, that she was so glad they had come to his hometown, and that she would always want to come back.

Chapter 5

"Come in Harold"

November 1

THE EXCITENENT OF the hole-in-one during the previous day's golf excursion, and the evening Halloween party with the Harold's Gibson City friends, had exhausted the couple, who, after making love, fell into a deep, relaxing sleep.

Harold awoke early, letting Akemi sleep in until he fixed breakfast and then tickled her feet until she opened her eyes, smiled, greeted the morning, and then Harold, with a kiss.

They had agreed the day before that she would relax at the house, put some final touches on her thesis, then go to his parent's home to show his mother the art of flower arranging, Ikebana, as Harold needed to talk to one more person before they left.

He did not mention it to Akemi, but Harold wanted an honest opinion from someone he trusted about his prospects for returning to the major leagues this year.

While Harold drove to his friend's house, he thought about how long he had known the man who would now realistically assess if, when, and how he could return to baseball at the highest level in the United States, and the world.

He trusted the man to be brutally honest about this situation, as was his style.

As he walked to the door of the small, white frame house in a town much smaller than his own hometown, Harold smiled and thought of the comments his host for the morning, Ernie White, had said to him over the years.

The comments had ranged from praise, to encouragement, to helpful suggestions, to schoolboy type lectures, and had always been on target.

Ernie was a baseball man through and through, one who knew what he was talking about, and one who was worth listening to when it came to advice for a ballplayer.

The hardened scout was a friend of his father's side of the family, had known about Gatewood's baseball abilities and potential from the time he was a boy in his early teen years, and had been the first scout to get a head start in the chase and following of the catcher as a developing prospect.

Gatewood had not signed when he was drafted by the veteran scout due to an injury in college.

The scout had always told Gatewood's father that his son had the best hands, arm, and defensive abilities of any catcher in the country.

He had always liked Gatewood's fast bat, natural power to right center field, the ability to handle what was asked of him, his intelligence and attitude, and being what the scout had said "the most competitive player I have ever seen."

A short, stout, bespectacled, left-handed man with an ever-present plastic cup at his side to catch the spittle from the constant wad of chewing tobacco which rested in his mouth, the scout would peer at the field, squint, then commit his notes to his mind.

White rarely wrote notes while at the ballpark, to conceal any possible interest in a prospect from watchful eyes, and to keep his interest level close to the vest, and unknown to other scouts.

He had respected the two generations of Gatewood catchers, playing against, and being good friends, with the father.

As a player, the scout himself had been a left-handed hitting infielder who could hit for high average, and enough power to satisfy whatever level of organized ball he was playing in at the moment.

Injuries had cut his career short, so he understood what Gatewood had been through, and was now currently dealing with, even though the disappointment was of a personal loss.

As a scout, he knew his business, and had made the rounds for many years with several different teams, which was the norm for a scout.

He had made one signing in his career, one which carried a high bonus, which did not pan out for the organization, and was labeled the fall guy for the player's failure to reach the major leagues.

The failure was the player's, and not the scout's, but the result was a change of scenery for the scout.

His signings had resulted in many players making it to the major leagues, including three batting champions, and two Hall of Fame inductees.

He was respected for his insight, knowledge, and ability to pick diamonds in the rough prospects by envisioning the potential, not the current events in a player's performance.

Harold knew he would be greeted at the door, enter the home where they would then head to the living room where Ernie could sit in his favorite rocking chair for their conversation.

He also knew they would eventually talk about Gatewood's grandfather, who was at most of his games from Little League through college, before he passed away.

The grandfather had a big, winning personality, and the scout had liked him very much.

While Harold waited on the screened in, front porch, a smile creeped on to his face as he waited for the scout to come to the door.

"Hello, Harold !"
"Hi, Ernie."
"Come in. Come in."
"Thanks."
"You remember my wife, Annabelle."
"Of course. It is nice to see you again."
"How are you?"
"I am feeling great. How are you two?"
"We are doing fine."
"You look great, like young lovebirds."
"Ha! We're passed the young part of that comment."
"You both look wonderful."
"How are your parents, Harold?"
"They are doing very well."
"I read where your dad caught a monster musky."
"Yes, we were together last year when he caught it."
"How big was it?"
"It was just over sixty pounds."
Unbelievable, what a fish!"
"It was the most exciting catch I have ever seen!"
"You did well in Japan last year.'
"Yes. I had a really good year."
"How is your arm?"
"It feels fine. I did not have any pain, and the strength is almost back."
"Did you catch any games?"
"No."
"Where did you play?"
"Mainly left field.'
"Did you like it?"
"Yes. I made a lot of progress in the position."
"Where else did you play?"
"I was in the infield, at first and third base.'
"Did you like it there?"
"Yes, first base was very easy."

"What about third base?"

"I really liked that position. My hands are still very good. I can play third base."

"What about your hitting?"

"It came back. I went back to my original style of hitting up the middle."

"You hit over .300?"

"Yes."

"What about your power?"

"It was good. It came back."

"You hit a lot of home runs?"

"Yes, to all fields. Thirty-six homer runs, Ernie. My power is back."

"What about the pitching in Japan?"

"Everyone says it is at a AAA plus level, but not at the major league level, and I agree with that assessment."

"What are the noticeable differences?"

"They usually use a six-man pitching rotation compared to our five-man rotation here. You face those number six starters over there."

"Did it make a big difference?"

"Yes, if the number six guy was a marked reduction in talent."

"Do you think you can ever catch again Harold?"

"Yes, I can. My arm is sound."

"How many games a year can you catch/'

If I limit my throwing, I can catch ninety to a hundred games."

"Would you be satisfied being a platoon player, in the lineup against left-handed pitching?"

"Yes, I will do anything they ask to get back into the big leagues."

"Can you still hit-left handed pitching?"

Gatewood smiled and said "I still tear them up."

"Would you be willing to catch, play left field, first base, third base, and pinch hit?"

"Yes, that is what I actually see myself doing right now."

"What about starting at the Triple A level and proving you belong in the majors again?"

"I would be fine with that if I could have some kind of agreement that I would be brought up if I produce at that level."

"I will see what I can do for you, Harold."

"Thanks Ernie. Will you do me a favor?"

"Sure."

"Please tell me my real chances of getting a major league contract?"

"It's not too good right now."

"What are their concerns?"

"Obviously, they want you as a catcher. You were the best catcher in the business for years."

"I understand."

"They are afraid of your arm. And, they are afraid that you will never want to sit down, as you are so competitive that you will not be happy sitting the bench."

"I understand both of those statements. I have matured a lot the last three years, and see my role differently now."

"When is your contract up in Japan?"

"It is up now. I am going to talk with them in a about ten days when I return to Japan."

"What kind of money did you make there?"

"I had a pretty good contract. I made good money."

"Give me a figure."

"I made several multiples of the figures they pay a good backup catcher her in the big leagues. I had a really good year, and they liked my contributions. I am expecting to get a really big raise. Plus, the endorsement money in Japan is a huge deal."

"How would it compare to a top flight catcher's compensation package here?"

"It would be less, but still good."

"If you could catch two more years like you used to you would get top dollar. But that might be hard to sell to them.

I think you would make as much or more, than you will be making in Japan.

But if you are arm is sound you will get a big contract. These days, no catcher throws out baserunners like you used to do."

"Thanks for that honest assessment. Ernie."

"You're welcome. There do have one other concern, Harold."

"What is it?"

"Over the last three years you have gone through events and tragedies that would have crippled many people's spirits. How are you really feeling?"

"I am fine. I will admit it has been tough, but I will not let it get me down."

"What actually happened in Spain?"

"What didn't. Ernie?"

"I heard that a terrorist group was after you."

'Yes, the AIO."

"Why?"

"I helped the Spanish government prevent a terrorist attack on a cultural landmark."

"No wonder they wanted to get even with you. Was there more to it?"
"Yes. They also had a serial killer on the loose."
"How were you involved in that?"
"I helped the police catch him, and solve a few murders."
"I heard that the King of Spain honored you as a hero."
"Yes, they honored my actions for helping save many lives."
"Harold, that was fantastic."
"Thanks. I just did what anyone would have done."
"Then you went to Cuba."
"Yes, to scout for major league baseball."
"What happened there?"
"I fell in love with the President of Cuba's secretary, and became involved as a target in an attempted coup to oust the president."
"And, someone tried to kill you?"
"Yes, the rebellious faction of the Cuban government tried to kill me. And, the AIO tried several times also."
"And, they murdered your fiancé?"
"Yes. I have lost two fiancés because of the AIO, one in Spain and one in Cuba."
"Harold, you have been through the wringer."
"I know. But I have learned a lot, and I am okay."
"Are you married now?"
"It is funny you asked. I just got engaged."
"Congratulations. Is she from here?"
"Thanks. No, she is from China."
"She must be a wonderful woman."
"Yes, she is."
"Harold, I want to tell you a couple more things."
"Okay."
"With all that has happened to you, if you are able to make it back to the big leagues, and taking into account all of the obstacles you will have overcome you will be a comeback story like no other, one which will make the turnstiles to the ballpark turn. Your story will be worth a lot to any team."
"Thank you, Ernie."
"How would you feel about that, if it would happen?"
"What do you mean?"
"Would you be willing to go through that, if you made a successful comeback?"
"Yes, if it would be handled in a way that would help the country in its fight against terrorism."

"There is one more thing Harold. "Maybe being overseas is not the best place for you and your family."

"I know."

"As your friend, I would urge you to think very seriously about that situation."

"Thank you. I will."

"Good. Is there anything else I can do for you Harold?"

"Just do me a favor, and let me know if there is an opportunity for me here in the United States."

"I will. Harold, you are almost back. Keep trying."

"Thanks, Ernie."

On the way back to Gibson City, Harold thought long and hard about what Ernie had told him.

He had a lot to consider, and would have a much better idea of his future once he returned to Tokyo, and had talked with the Tokyo Giants.

Chapter 6

To the Tokyo Dome

November 15

THE LAST DAYS of the Illinois visit continued to be ones of relaxation, which saw Akemi work with Harold's mother on various craft projects, and Harold spend time with his dad at the golf course.

Also included was a short fishing trip to Michigan by the entire family, which targeted steelhead, brown trout, and walleye, in the St. Joseph and Muskegon Rivers.

The steelhead run had just started, with fresh fish entering the rivers from the Great Lakes each day. Catches were in the fifteen-to-twenty-pound range, of the hard fighting Skamania steelhead species.

It had been a grand trip, with everyone being comfortable with the news that Harold and Akemi would soon be a couple who would start their lives together.

Harold had told his parents that he would finalize his contract with the Tokyo Giants for the coming year as soon as they returned to Japan, and that the couple would then head to Beijing to meet Akemi's parents.

He told his parents that he would be buying their ticket to China, as a thank you for all that they had done for him.

The apartment in Tokyo looked small after staying in Harold's home in Illinois, but it was home for the moment, and it was good that the long flight was over.

The couple arrived late in the evening, and did not even bother to unpack, instead going to bed, making love, and then falling asleep.

Harold's appointment with his manager, Katashi Katsu, was set for two in the afternoon.

Harold would plan on staying with the Cardinals the following year, as he liked Japanese baseball, the money was good, and he and Akemi were comfortable in Tokyo.

He would require that his contract would include an escape clause if he would be picked up by a team in the major leagues during the upcoming season.

If that occurred, he would sign a new contract with the team in the United States for more money.

The Cardinals would be compensated by selling him to the American team, so Harold did not anticipate any problems on the inclusion of that clause in his contract.

Harold was interested in hearing the terms and dollar value of the new contract, as he had done everything the organization had asked of him, and more.

He knew what his worth to the club was, and had a figure in mind. In his career, he had been compensated well, based on his performance and the fact that he had two excellent negotiators in his corner, his agent Randle Quinn, and his dad.

Harold had spoken with his agent, and had been briefed on what he should expect. He liked the organization, and felt confident they would treat him fairly.

Harold kissed Akemi, teased her that he wished she would have let him do that the first time he had seen her doing her Tai Chi exercises in the courtyard in front of the apartment building months before, and headed down the street toward the Tokyo Dome.

As he walked, Harold thought about the many trips he had made during the previous season, and all that had transpired since he had arrived in Tokyo.

He also thought about his first trip to the Tokyo Dome, after settling into the city and his apartment, when he had met the team personnel, his teammates, and his new manager.

Memories of the first time he had met the beautiful Kimiko Michi Hayato flooded his mind when he reached the point where she had pulled her red sports car to the curb and asked him for his autograph.

He then remembered the nights of passion, the inability to convince her that there was nothing between them, her failed suicide attempt for which her parents blamed him, her visiting him at his hotel room on a road trip, her selling drugs to his teammates, and her failed murder attempt on the woman he loved, Akemi.

Harold also remembered the result of Kimiko's drug sales, which manifested itself in Mario Kennedy's suicide leap from the hotel patio which he and teammate Scott Binder could not prevent.

The follow up actions of Kimiko's Yakuza crime family also entered his mind.

The poisoning of his teammate Jim Lockwood, which was intended for Harold himself, was recalled as Harold walked.

The shootout near the retail stores along the street, in which Harold survived, and which led to the deaths of the Yakuza assassins, and the death of the AIO assassin Bittor Kemen was memorable, but not enjoyable.

Most of all, he remembered how he had looked forward to seeing Akemi doing her exercises each, morning, seeing her finally smile at him the first time, he handing her his business card to introduce himself and asking permission from her father to ask her for a date.

He also remembered his actions of bringing her little gifts from the ballpark like the free t-shirt from the Ueno Zoo which celebrated the pandas Ri-Ri and Shin-Shun. and the first time she had said "Hai", which had led their first time making love.

His life in Tokyo had taken many turns, but was one in which he was now blessed. As he approached the front entrance to the dome, he was grateful, and looked forward to continuing to be a Cardinal for another year.

"Hello, Harold."

"Hello, Skip."

"Please come in."

"Thanks."

"How was your trip to America ?"

"It was enjoyable."

"Did Akemi like it?"

"Yes. She had a very nice time."

"How did the meeting between your parents and Akemi go?"

"Wonderfully, well. They liked each other very much."

"Great."

"I am glad to be back, Skip."

"I am glad you came in today."

"I like it here so it is always nice to come in."

"We need to talk about your future with the club."

"Great."

"Harold, when I met you at the World Games in Cuba two years ago, I knew you were a professional, and that you would help us here."

"Thank you."

"You surpassed every expectation we had for you."

"Thanks."

"Your defensive was good."

"I was very comfortable in left field."

"Your arm came around."

"Yes, I appreciated you helping me with the acupuncture treatments. They were very helpful."

"We were extremely pleased with your power, as you hit many more home runs than we expected."

"I did think that changing my hitting style led to that."

"Your runs batted in, and your batting average were both very pleasant surprises."

"Yes, I was also pleased with those numbers."

"We loved your leadership.

"Thanks Skip."

"You always hustled, and gave us your all."

"Thanks. That is the only way I know how to play."

"When we brought you here, he wanted you to bring the intangibles with you. We knew you would teach our younger players how to act and play professionally. You did an outstanding job in that area."

"It was my pleasure to do so."

"In these contract negotiations, my hands are tied, other than giving my input on all of the items we have discussed today."

"I understand."

"Sometimes, my input is acknowledged as correct, and sometimes it is not."

"I know how those discussions take place."

"In this one, with you, the owners and upper management did not take my recommendations."

"I have been in the same position, Skip."

"As hard as I tried for you, I failed to convince the bean counters of your total value."

"I understand, and I appreciate you going to bat for me."

"In my position, as you know, some things are dictated to me."

"I know."

"In this case, I pushed as hard as I could, perhaps even too far, at risk to my leadership position, for your contributions."

"I appreciate that."

"Harold, it gives me great pain to tell you that upper management has decided not to renew your contract with the Tokyo Giants."

The words stunned Harold, causing him to sit silently for a moment while the decision could be processed in his brain.

He was not sure he had heard correctly. He also thought that his manager might be playing a joke on him.

He didn't know what to do, other than sit silently. The Giants' manager broke the awkward situation by saying that he would do what he could for Harold.

"Harold, I think you are ready to rejoin a team in the Major Leagues, in America."

"Thank you, Skip. I would appreciate your help in getting signed somewhere."

"I will do all I can for you."

"What options do you think are out there for me?"

"You may have to go back to the states ad play in AAA."

"Okay."

"I think that other teams in our Nippon Baseball League would sign you, for less money."

"Okay."

"Also, the professional league in Korea might have an interest in you."

"I understand."

"There are two other options for you."

"What are they?"

"China. The Chinese Professional League in Taiwan will sign you. I think you will have better options than this though."

Okay."

"The other league on mainland China is the China Gold League. We enjoy a good working relationship with them in regards to player development."

"How does the league really compare to here in Tokyo?"

"It is not as good frankly, but it an option, and you would do very well there. You would be scouted."

"I would appreciate all that you can do for me."

"I think your release is a disgrace, Harold, but I can't say that publicly or I will be fired."

"Was there anything else which led to me being released?"

"You never heard from me what I am going to tell you."

"Okay."

"The franchise has had many scandals. In 2004 we were fined for scouting violations, and for paying money to amateurs as an incentive to eventually sign with us."

"I heard about that."

"In 2012 the manager had an extra martial affair. The team paid blackmail hush money to the Yakuza to keep the scandal quiet. After that, a new manger was hired."

"I remember that."

"This year, there were the gambling associations with the Yakuza, Mario Kennedy's drug-related, suicide, the poisoning of Jim Lockwood by the

Yakuza, and your association with Kimiko Hayato, the second-in-command with the Yakuza crime family."

"What else impacted the decision to let me go?"

"The team is owned by the Ying Communications Group. They have been put in a poor position by the events I mentioned."

"I understand that."

"They were also sensitive to global politics, and the relations between Japan and China in the South China Sea over the Senkaku Islands made them uneasy.'

"How?"

"I told them that it is none of their business, but they felt it was a problem that you were involved with your girlfriend, who happens to be the daughter of the Vice-President of China."

"That is none of their business."

"I agree, Harold. But I lost the argument."

"I appreciate you going to bat for me."

"It wasn't your on-field, play, Harold. It was the series of events which took place this season, most of which had nothing to do with you."

"Not to be nosey Skipper, but where do you stand with the organization."

"I am on thin ice. If things go badly this year I will be out."

"I wish you the best. You are a very good manager and I enjoyed playing for you."

"I wish you were coming back here, Harold."

"It's just business. Maybe we will be on the same team again someday."

"Good luck, Harold."

Harold went to the business office to sign the needed forms, and then headed to the locker room to clear out his locker. He was surprised to see his roommate, Scott Binder also cleaning out his locker.

"Scott, what happened?"

"I was released."

"Me too."

"Harold, I had a down year so I wasn't that surprised about being let go. But you were fantastic, and should have been signed by the major leagues, and been on your way to America the last half of the season."

"Thanks, Scott. What are you going to do?"

"I will try to hook on with someone. What about you?"

"I am in the same boat as you."

"When you get signed by someone put in a good word for me."

"I will. Please do the same for me."

"Of course. Maybe we will be teammates again."

"I hope so, Scott."

Harold cleaned out his locker, and started the walk back to the apartment. It would be a different walk than any before during his time in Tokyo.

Harold wasn't bitter, or upset, but he was still surprised, and hurt. He focused his thoughts on what he had accomplished during the past year, the comments from Pat Sullivan, Ernie White, and most of all, from his dad.

He knew he was close to making a successful comeback to the major leagues.

When he would arrive at the apartment he would tell Akemi of the events of the day, and then call his agent to tell him the news.

They had planned on moving as his comeback continued so this would just be an early start on the continuation of that journey.

The best part was that he was not making it alone, but with the one woman he truly loved.

Chapter 7

Meet The Parents

November 30

HAROLD HAD CALLED his agent, Randle Quinn, to inform him of his release from the Tokyo Giants, and to ask him to start to look for other options for the next season.

He instructed Randle to check with every major league team to see if they were interested in signing him.

He also told Randle that he would consider any offer which would get him to the major leagues, but that he wanted a decent contract, and a written clause that he would be called up to the parent club if he started out in the minors.

Harold knew that a written guarantee was probably not attainable, but that it would lead to a gentleman's unwritten agreement if he would produce on the field.

He also knew that it would give his agent negotiating room, and would give an immediate indication of what every team thought of his comeback chances.

Harold knew he belonged back in major league baseball, and wanted every club to know that he was willing to fill whatever role they might need.

Gatewood also wanted to get the details of his next contract completed as soon as possible, as he did not want to wait until the last minute before the season started to know who might have interest in his possible contributions.

He also discussed the possibility of playing outside the United States once again, if the major league clubs would not sign him.

He had an idea of where he could go, and felt confident that there were three other certain possibilities, and one additional possible option if he would not hook on with a team in America.

Akemi had reacted with her total support, as he knew she would. She told him she wanted to be with him, no matter where they would live, and no matter what he would be doing, baseball or not.

She also told him she would stay in Japan if he signed with another Nippon League team, but that she was actually ready for a change of scenery if Japan was not an option.

Since Harold was not going to be a Tokyo Cardinal next year, he would have to vacate his apartment. Akemi's apartment lease was up the end of November, and he had moved in with her for the last two weeks of the month.

Packing would be easy, as Harold had lived like a single ballplayer, with few clothes and possessions to cart around, as a ballplayer, at many times in his career, unfortunately did not know the certainty of his next contract, or if he would be released.

Akemi lived like a college student, also having few clothes and possessions, which would make her part of the move also an easy one.

The couple had talked about where to live in the timeframe when Harold would be looking for another team for which to play. Harold wanted to meet her parents, and ask her father for permission to marry Akemi.

His suggestion was to stay in Beijing and rent a small furnished apartment on a month-to-month lease until the contract issue was addressed.

Akemi was delighted with his suggestion, as she wanted to see her parents and start their married lives on familiar turf.

They would fly to Beijing, each carrying their belongings with them in one suitcase, a gym bag, and a computer bag. They had laughed at how easy the packing for the move had been.

They would stay with Akemi's parents for a few days, then finalize their housing and transportation needs, with Akemi staying at her parents as an engaged woman, until the wedding.

The lovebirds planned on getting married in a matter of days, taking a short honeymoon in the country, and then settling down in the apartment.

They knew that her parents were not prudes, but both of them wanted to honor Akemi's parents, and the traditional Chinese martial customs.

The flight was enjoyable, as the couple talked about her parents, and what Harold should expect when they would meet.

Naturally, Harold was a bit nervous, but knew he would make a good first impression, and was determined to be his usual confident, pleasant self.

He knew that Akemi had informed her parents on his background, and the fact that she thought he was the personification of the ideal man who would be her life partner.

Yong Wei would also accompany them to China, where he would continue to be Akemi's bodyguard. Cramped into the economy seat of the plane, he had fallen asleep as soon as he had determined that there was no danger on the plane.

He was a single man, with no family, so his assignment of protecting Akemi was one which he enjoyed. He had served her father for many years, and had a natural affection for the family.

He had seen Akemi grow up and become a wonderful young woman. He had also seen the never-ending line of suitors who wanted to marry Akemi, some of whom he had liked, and many of which he had not liked.

He respected Harold as a man, and knew that his love for her was real, based on how he treated her.

The bodyguard was happy to be returning to China, as he had missed his home country, and was also certain that the couple would be safer in Beijing.

Akemi's parents were at the airport to greet the couple, her mother furiously waving at them as they headed from the plane to the area beyond the security gate. Her father was smiling, but not waving, as he had an image to maintain due to his position in the Chinese government.

Her mother was a short, five-foot one-inch, dark haired, attractive woman of Japanese origin.

Her father was a small bodied man, five-foot eight inch in height, with dark hair, and light-colored rimmed glasses.

Akemi was waving to her parents, a smile which ran from one corner of her beautiful mouth to the other resting on her face. She hugged and kissed her parents and then introduced Harold to her parents.

"Father, mother, this is Harold Gatewood, the man I love."

Harold bowed as best as he could, then shook both parents' hands, and said in Chinese that he was very glad to meet them, that Akemi had told him many nice things about them, and that it was obvious where she got her nice qualities.

The comments seemed to break whatever consternation might have existed, and the couple smiled broadly in approval to what they had just heard.

The couple, and the parents, talked freely as they walked toward the exit of the terminal. A military escort had accompanied her parents, one which provided the needed protection of her father, the Vice President of China.

The military men would gather the couple's luggage, and load them into the car for the trip to the government residence provided for a man of her father's position.

Akemi's mother had met the man who would become her husband while she was in China as a college student, a fact which did not go unnoticed by Harold.

At the time of their meeting, Akemi's Father had been an intelligence officer in the military.

Later, due to stellar performance in his field, he would be chosen to enter the political area, and had rapidly moved up through the chairs of the Communist Party to his present position as Vice President.

Both of Akemi's parents were educated at the master's level. Her mother's field of study was mathematics, an area which attested to her analytical ability.

Her father's specialties were in the areas of Organizational Planning and Political Science, both which had proved to be of great value in his military and political careers.

They had quickly asked Akemi how close she was to finishing her master's degree, to which she had stated that she was done, and needed only to send her thesis to the university on Tokyo to be read and approved.

She had told her parents that Harold had been a great help to her in the final stages of the completion of her thesis.

Akemi also told her parents that Harold had his doctoral degree, with dissertation topics of the career training and motivation of professional athletes.

Her father was very interested in the topic and asked Harold to cover the basics of his study.

Upon hearing the details of the dissertation, and the how they had been accepted and used by major league baseball in America, her father said that he could see value in the program in the China Baseball League and Chinese Olympic athletes, and that he would like to talk to him about it later.

Her father also told Harold that he had seen him play his last game in America, against the New York Yankees, when he had been on a state visit to America.

He told Harold, "In the game, I saw you strike out two times."

After exploding in laughter, Harold replied "Those things happened, more often than I would like to admit."

Akemi's father further teased Harold. "You also made an error, by throwing the ball away at third base when a runner tried to steal. He then came home."

Harold laughed again. "Luckily, that didn't happen that often, but it did that time."

Harold liked her parents, and the feelings were mutual.

Akemi later told him that she had hoped for a quick acceptance by her parents, and that the result of the first meeting could not have been better.

After settling into the residence for the night, Akemi kissed Harold goodnight, laughed, and said how funny it was that she was heading to different bedrooms.

She then said that she wanted to sneak back into Harold's room later, but that it would be too dangerous, as the Vice-President's residence was video monitored for security reasons.

The next day before supper, Harold had an opportunity to speak with Akemi's father, and asked if he could have permission to marry he and his wife's daughter.

The answer was a definite yes.

Harold was relieved, and when he and her father entered the home's living room, Akemi looked at her father, who broke out into a broad smile, and said "Congratulations Akemi, your mother and I are gaining a son-in-law. We wish you both all of the happiness in the world."

The couple set a wedding date of December 15th. They would have ample time to plan the wedding, as Akemi had already put much thought into the type of ceremony she wanted.

She had chosen a traditional Chinese wedding, and had already mentally addressed the needed items and traditions for the ceremony.

Harold called his parents, told them the news, and the date of the ceremony.

He also told them that he had already purchased their tickets to Beijing, made arrangements for their lodging, and reminded them that it was winter, and cold, in Beijing, so warm clothing would be needed.

In the two weeks before the ceremony Harold would finalize the renting of the furnished apartment, he and Akemi would call home, rent a car, buy a Winter coat, hat, scarf, and gloves to braze the cold, plan a honeymoon location, find time to work out, monitor the progress of his agent's efforts regarding his possible baseball contract in America, and see some of the Beijing sites with Akemi.

He had never visited China, and was anxious to see some of what the country had to offer.

The country was vast, with grasslands, deserts, mountains, rivers, lakes, and a long ocean coastline. The weather was varied, spread over five zones, each with a different temperate makeup.

One area would be classified by cold, one by a mid- temperate climate, another by a warm weather pattern, yet another by a subtropical pattern of weather, and lastly, one area was blessed with a tropical climate.

The northern part of the country, where Beijing was located, endured monsoons, and cold, below zero temperatures in the winter, much like Illinois.

The summers were marked by temperatures above sixty-eight degrees, often to very high levels of heat.

Rainfall in the country increased as one traveled from the southeast to the northwest part of China.

May through September was characterized by rain, except in the coastal areas of the country.

The summer monsoon rains came from the West Pacific Ocean and Southwest Indian Ocean breezes. One nasty weather feature in Beijing was the abundance of smog, which Harold thought would be very hard for the baseball players to endure.

Akemi's father invited she and Harold to see where he, the Vice President, worked, called the Zhongnanhi.

The building was located next to the Forbidden City in Central Beijing.

His office was in the central headquarters of the Communist Party of China building, the State Council for the People's Republic of China. The building was between the Central and Southern Lakes to the West of the Forbidden City.

The Xinhuamen, or Gate of New China, was at the South entrance to the compound.

It was complete with quotes which honored the Communist Party, "Long live the great Communist Party of China", and past Chairman Mao Zedong, "Long live invincible Mao Zedong thought", and his reproduced quote in his personal handwriting "Serve the people".

The office of the Vice-President, the Guojia Fuzhuki or State vice-Chairman, was created by the 1982 Constitution.

Akemi's father was in his first, elected, five-year, term, and was eligible for election to a second five-year stint. The election was carried out by the National People's Congress, which was the national legislature of the country.

His duties were to assist the president of the country, replace the president if he should die or leave office, serve as Secretary of the Communist Party Committee and the Politburo Standing Committee and Central Secretariat, the decision, making body of the government.

Her Father was in charge of the party workings, sat on the Foreign Affairs Leading Group, had a leading role in foreign affairs, and enjoyed high prestige and political power.

After lunch Akemi took Harold on a tour of the Forbidden City, the one, hundred, eighty, acre, Forbidden Palace complex which housed almost one thousand buildings.

Harold enjoyed the Gate of Heavenly Purity, which was the outer main gate entrance to the complex, the Palace of Heavenly Purity, the Hall of Union, the Palace of Earthly Tranquility, the Inner Court, which was the palace of the Emperor, the Meridian Gate, and the Gate of Divine Might.

After a break for bottles of water, and a few "I love you" comments, the couple continued on their personal tour, weeing the East and West Glorious Gates, the unique Corner Towers, the Gate and Hall of Supreme Harmony, the hall of Military Eminence, the Hall of Literary Glory, the Hall of Mental Cultivation, the Palace of Tranquility, and the Imperial Gardens.

The couple was getting tired of sightseeing, and exited the Forbidden City into Tiananmen Square, a vast open area which was home to the National Museum of China on one side, the Great Hall of the People on the other side, with the Monument of the Heroes and the Mao Zedong Mausoleum on one end of the square.

The square also was home to the Zhengyang Men, which displayed the history of the city of Beijing.

Tiananmen Square was the site of the student protests of June third and fourth, in 1981, which caused the government to use force on the demonstrators to stop the riot.

Martial law was declared and the uprising was crushed.

Harold told Akemi about two similar occurrences in United States history which happened during the Civil War.

President Abraham Lincoln quelled the uprising of April 19, 1861 in Baltimore, Maryland by the suspending the writ of habeas corpus, which guaranteed individual rights, in an attempt to preserve order and prevent destruction of the railroads which were needed to transport Union troops during the war.

Lincoln also ignored the Supreme Court ruling overturning his actions, then arrested and jailed political opponents without trial, and jailed newspaper and book authors who did not support his war efforts, in direct violation of the Constitution.

"Honest Abe" Lincoln was not the only President in the Civil war to suspend individual rights through suspension of habeas corpus. The President of the Confederacy, Jefferson Davis, also did so in order to preserve domestic order.

As Harold and Akemi sat on a bench outside, huddling close for warmth, they talked about how different their cultures had been over the years, and about the miracle that brought them together.

"It is hard to find one's soul mate, and neither one of the couples
   had ever imagined that their one and only would come from a country so far away from where they had spent their childhood".

Harold did want to learn how Akemi's father had raised to the powerful position he now held, and had several questions.

"Akemi, how did your father get into politics?"

"He was a very good intelligence officer in the army, and made several recommendations on how to change and reorganize the way in which the military made decisions."

"He was a visionary?"

"Yes, he had a unique way of looking at a situation, seeing a solution, and convincing others that his plan was the best way to solve the problem."

"He was a skilled politician from early on?"

"Yes. He had a natural ability to say and do the right thing in a way that would allow him to get what he wanted without alienating others who wanted something different.

He was shrewd, and well-liked. He rose up through the ranks quickly."

"That is a rare skill."

"Yes, my grandfather always tried to use the principle that negotiation must be done in a manner such that he would get what he wanted yet left the other person thinking he got what he wanted."

"He is a sharp guy."

"Does he have any political enemies?"

"Only one."

"Min Jun."

"Why does he dislike your father?"

"He dislikes him for many reasons."

"Personal reasons?"

"Yes. He and my father were both in love with my mother from the first time they both saw her."

"I can understand that. She must have been very beautiful."

"Yes, she was."

"And she chose to marry your father rather than Min Jun."

"Yes."

"Are there other reasons?".

"Yes, political ones."

"Such as?"

"Min Jun and my father have always been political rivals, vying for the same positions, and offices."

"And your father always wins."

"Almost always."

"Do they have different makeups??"

"Yes, my father is very reserved and uses people skills and diplomacy to reach his goals, while Min Jun uses sledgehammer type techniques to intimidate and bully his opponents to reach his goals."

"He sounds like a charmer."

"He is very dangerous, and will do anything to try to get what he wants."

"Is there trouble brewing between them on important issues?"

"Yes, on practically everything as it relates to the future path the country will take."

"What do you think will happen?"

"My father is next in line to become President of the country. Min Jun will vie for the same office."

"Who do you think will win?"

"My father has been building relationships with the right people, and will be elected as the next president."

"What will happen then?"

"Min Jun is very vindictive. If my father is to become to the next President, which should be several years from now, as he had seven more years as Vice President, then that election will be a very hard fought one."

"Will Min Jun ever accept defeat?"

"I don't think so. I think he will try to sabotage my father's efforts for the country every day he is alive, as he is doing now."

"He sounds like a bitter, deranged man."

"Yes, he is ruthless, and somewhat touched."

"At least your father made one good negotiation."

"What was that?"

"Winning, and marrying your mother."

"Yes, we all are glad for that."

"I am too, otherwise I would have never met you."

"That is very sweet, Harold."

"Good negotiations are catching. I made one when I got you."

"And, I got one when you asked me to marry you."

"It was the best decision of my life honey. I love you."

"I love you too, Harold."

Chapter 8

"Of course, I do."

December 15

THE TWO WEEKS SINCE the couple's arrival had passed quickly, with the meeting of Akemi's parents, the settling in to the new apartment, the visiting of many of Beijing's historical sites, and the making of final arrangements for Harold's parents' tickets and travel details to China for the wedding, being accomplished.

They would stay in Harold's apartment during the days before and after the wedding. Harold had made plans for them to meet Akemi's parents, after which the two families would be involved in final wedding details.

The couple had been able to spend time together, do their Tai Chi exercises, work out, and steak away quiet moments together for lovemaking each day.

Harold was keeping in good shape, readying himself for whatever direction his career would head in the upcoming months.

Akemi had introduced him to her childhood friends from Beijing, and had shown him where she had lived in the city during her youth.

Harold and Akemi had driven to the airport to pick up his parents on their day of arrival. As they waited in the front area of the airport, they wagered on how big a smile his parents would have on their faces when they cleared customs and would see the couple waiting for them.

After hugs and kisses, the family enjoyed the drive through the city to the apartment, after which they talked about how happy they were for the couple, and about more day-to-day events in America.

Akemi had fixed the evening meal, which could be reheated, as she knew from checking the flight schedule, their trip from Central Illinois to Chicago O'Hare, then to Beijing, would have been a long, tiring one characterized by jet lag.

Harold had stocked the refrigerator and cupboards with more food than his parents could eat in three weeks, let alone ten days. Everything had been arranged for their comfort during the stay in China, including written instructions on how to use the television remote control unit.

Harold would stay with his parents at the apartment, and Akemi would stay with her parents, until the day of the wedding.

After acclimating to the time change, where Beijing was fourteen hours, and one day on the calendar, ahead of Illinois time, his parents were ready to meet Akemi's parents the following day. Everyone would meet at the residence of the Vice-President, and become acquainted.

Harold's Mother had brought pictures of him from the time he was a boy, until the present day, and snapshots of the couple's home in Illinois, to show Akemi's parents a glimpse of their family history and life in America.

Included in the pictures were framed enlargements of two pictures of Harold and Akemi during her visit to Gibson City, Illinois, which she gave to Akemi's parents as a present.

The first picture was of the couple in front of the three-story fireplace in Harold's family room, and second was of the couple in front of Harold's home.

His mother then said she wanted Akemi's parents to have them because the couple looked so much in love, and that she wanted Akemi's parents to be able to look at the picture an always know the depth of the couple's commitment.

After the gift was presented, Akemi's Mother handed a wrapped gift to Harold's mother, when after it was opened, caused both families to erupt in hilarious laughter.

The gift was a framed picture of Harold and Akemi, standing in front of the entrance to the Forbidden City, arms around each other, and looking very much in love.

The exchange of the same type of gift was an unexpected occurrence, but one which was not only humorous, but was one which permanently broke the ice in terms of the sets of parents liking each other.

Harold's parents were very dignified, possessed qualities of high character, had outgoing, big personalities, and were very easy to like.

Akemi's parents, in typical Chinese cultural mores, were more reserved, but were very likeable, and pleasant, once they were confident, they could accept and trust a person. They were gracious hosts and very soon, both couples were enjoying themselves, seemly not noticing Harold and Akemi's presence.

Harold and Akemi were able to drift away for a moment in another room where they enjoyed a few kisses and talked in private.

"Harold, I am so proud of you. You father and mother even removed their shoes when they entered the residence."

"I know honey. I had to remind them of that before we all arrived."

"I am so glad that they recognized that Chinese custom."

"It is different in that respect form ours, but we all want everything to go smoothly during their visit."

"It is working out great. And, we will be able to be alone for a few minutes, as they seem to have forgotten us."

"I know. Isn't it wonderful?"

Akemi's parents arranged for an official tour of the Vice-President's workplace, the President's office, the governmental offices, and the Forbidden City, and rolled out the red carpet for their visit.

This gracious act allowed Harold and Akemi time to be alone, talk, and make love in the apartment the following days.

The five remaining days before the ceremony would allow both mothers of the couple to work on wedding items which would further make the day special.

Both ladies were artistic and creative, which made the job enjoyable and rewarding for both of them.

Harold and Akemi would be busy creating the wedding album, which would be modeled after recent trends in China which included pictures of the bride and groom at various locations, but none of the actual ceremony.

A photographer was hired to take pictures in front of the Vice President's office location in honor of the bride's father, in Tiananmen Square, and locations within the Forbidden City.

Akemi chose her favorite locations in the Forbidden City including the Gate of Supreme Harmony, the Palace of Heavenly Purity, the Palace of Earthly Tranquility, the Hall of Union, and many locations in the Imperial Gardens.

She also chose the Temple of Heaven, which was located in the southeastern part of Beijing, as she had always liked the architecture of the building, and its prayer to Heaven, the Tiantan.

The wedding of the couple, the daughter of the Vice-President of China and the famous baseball player from America, had attracted the interest of the Chinese people.

As a special surprise for Harold, Akemi had accepted an offer from the Beijing Tigers of the China Gold League, to use their home stadium, Huncheng Field for wedding pictures.

The couple had pictures taken with their arms around each other at home plate, on the home dugout steps, and in left field.

Harold was in full Beijing Tigers uniform and Akemi was in shots worn by the team's cheerleaders, and a uniform jersey.

On the way home the couple laughed at the irony of being pictured in a team uniform which he was not affiliated with, and talked about the options of where he would be playing the coming season.

Harold commented on the pictures, saying, "I bet my agent Scott Randle will have a stroke when he sees that picture. If that doesn't get the baseball world alerted to my availability, then nothing will."

The next day, Harold's parents accompanied them to another picture location for the wedding album, the Great Wall of China, a daytrip from Beijing.

Everyone was amazed at the magnificence of the structure, with its architectural features, and use for communication, the transporting of troops from one area of the country to another, its military presence of cannons and towers, which were located two arrow shots away from each other.

Built during the Ming dynasty it offered breathtaking views of the countryside, and served as a perfect location for the couple's wedding pictures.

Akemi had Harold meet her childhood best friend who would serve as her maid of honor in the wedding. Harold's best man would be his father.

As the wedding drew closer, the list of "to do's" grew shorter until they disappeared. The interest in the country for the wedding of the Vice-President grew each day.

Soon, it was an item of national news, a situation the couple had not asked, or bargained, for, and one which made the privately oriented couple who preferred to enjoy their own company as compared to the spotlight, somewhat uncomfortable.

The wedding would be a traditional Chinese one, with the seven steps of the couple's commitment to spend their lives together, would be as closely followed as possible.

The first step of etiquette in the wedding, the proposal by a matchmaker, had not happened, as the couple had met and fallen in love on their own.

The second step was addressed when Harold and Akemi visited a suan ming, a Chinese fortune teller, who predicted the future of the couple, based on their birthdays, to be one of long happiness and love.

The third step of the process was the betrothal of gifts from the groom to the bride's parents for their daughter's hand in marriage. Akemi's parents had told Harold that they had been blessed, were wealthy, and did not want monetary items for Akemi's hand, but wanted something from his heart to prove he loved their daughter.

Harold gave them an engraved plaque with the inscription that read:

"In honor of you granting me your daughter Akemi in marriage, I give you my word as a gentleman that I will always honor her, respect her, take care of her, protect her, provide for her, listen to her opinions, honor her family and cultural roots, and love her with all of my heart as long as I shall live. Harold Gatewood"

It was a simple plaque, and a short promise of fifty, two words, but one in which he had promised to be the husband who her parents had always wanted for their only daughter, their only child, Akemi.

Her parents knew that this promise was from Harold's heart, and that he would honor Akemi. It was the best gift they could have ever wanted.

The fourth step was the wedding gifts from the groom to the bride's family. Harold arranged for the traditional layout of food, cakes, and religious oriented gifts to the family, all of which were outlined for Harold by Akemi.

All items and gifts were gloriously appreciated and well received.

The fifth step was the arranging of the wedding in traditional Chinese style, which had been handled by the mothers of the bride and groom in the days leading up to the day of the wedding.

The last step of the process was the wedding ceremony itself.

The president of the country, and the State Council, the executive branch, the National People's Congress, the legislative branch, the Supreme People's Court, the judicial branch of the government, and the Communist Party of China all invited the couple to have their wedding ceremony inside the Forbidden City.

The wedding would not be held in the area which had been used for the past Emperors' weddings but would be conducted in a large hall which would befit the occasion.

Only one official, Min Jun, Akemi's father's bitter personal and political rival, opposed the action, on the grounds that it violated tradition.

There were three traditional steps in the ceremony.

A procession from the bride's parent's home to the groom's home and the presentation of the dowry to the bride's family was accomplished in fine fashion.

The second step was the welcoming of the bride at the door of the groom's home was also done.

The families then proceeded to the Forbidden City, as the wedding would take place there, thanks to the gracious acts of the Chinese government, and as a sign of respect to Akemi's father, who was Vice-President, was greatly respected.

Since the wedding had attracted national attention, the families were greeted by several thousand Chinese citizens when they reach Tiananmen Square, which caused some concern for the couple as they had wanted a quiet wedding which matched their lifestyle.

The reception was overwhelming as the wedding party was escorted through crowd into Forbidden City, then into the wedding hall.

The wedding ceremony itself was one of importance, where respect was aid to the emperor of the country.

The steps of the process included the exchange of nuptial cups, and a series of bows. The first bow was made to the honor of Heaven and earth, the second to the honor of the couple's ancestors, the third to the honor of the couple's parents, and the fourth was to the honor of each spouse to the other.

After the bows and the nuptial cups, Harold and Akemi spoke their vows, and pledged their love for each other. After a long kiss, the couple turned and walked down the aisle.

Akemi, dressed in a traditional log red dress, was beautiful. Harold looking splendid and dashing, was in a tuxedo.

Even as they walked down the aisle, Harold could not keep his eyes off of Akemi, as she was everything he had ever wanted in a wife.

The feeling was mutual, as Akemi loved everything about Harold, and was pledged to honor him as his wife.

The bride and groom's families were both overjoyed, as they knew that their children had found their significant only, and would enjoy a long, happy, loving life together.

Each thought brought back the happiness and memories of love and commitment they had enjoyed when they had married their own spouses.

The banquet after the ceremony, the xi-jiu, was an important event in which the families of the bride and groom, the guests at the wedding, would offer their nest wishes for happiness to the couple. It was also a time for the couple to enjoy themselves, and relax.

Near the end of the banquet, the couple would thank everyone for their attendance, and get ready to leave on their honeymoon.

They talked with Akemi's parents, who unbeknown to them, the couple would be spending their honeymoon at the same location their parents had when they had gotten married, and where her father had served in the military, Lintong District, Xian, Shaanxi Province.

The location was also the site of the mausoleum and museum of the first Emperor of China, Qin Shi Huang, and the archeological find of the Terra Cotta Army.

They would also visit with Harold's parents, wish them well, and tell them that Harold had arranged for their transportation to the airport on their departure date.

Akemi promised that they would visit them in Gibson City from wherever they would be, as soon as Harold's upcoming season was over.

They would spend their wedding night at a hotel near the airport, then fly to Xian early the next morning. It had been a grand occasion, and a wonderful day.

Akemi and Harold were relieved that the excitement and commotion of the day was over, and that they could now officially relax and enjoy their lives together as husband and wife.

After making love multiple times, the couple told each other that they loved each other, and exhausted, looked forward to a good night's sleep. Before dozing off, Harold wanted to talk to Akemi.

"Did you think everyone enjoyed the wedding?"

"Yes, I think both of our parents were very pleased."

"Were you surprised with the large turnout of the Chinese citizens who showed up at Tiananmen Square to show respect for our wedding?"

"Yes, I was completely surprised."

"Did you notice what I did at the wedding hall?"

"What was that, Harold?"

"It was about the president of China."

"What was it?"

"His pants were too long; just like in the picture we first saw in Tokyo."

"Harold, quit teasing me."

"Okay. Honey, did you really think that all of my bowing to you in Tokyo, when I was trying to get you to notice me, would lead to this?"

"Yes Harold. I had it all planned out."

"Was my bowing technique better during the ceremony today better than my first attempts in Tokyo?"

"They were perfect, darling."

'I love you Akemi. Do you love me?"

"Of course, I do."

Chapter 9

"What are my options?"

December 23

THE HONEYMOON HAD been great, as the Terra Cotta Army exhibit was very interesting, and the couple had time to relax together, and make love on a non-stop basis.

Akemi had not seen the exhibit, now a UNESCO World Heritage Site, since she was a teenager, and Harold had only seen the exhibit on loan in San Francisco.

The detail and craftsmanship one the eight thousand warriors, was etched into their faces, hair, shoes, and the articles of clothes and armor they wore. Each face was different, as if a human had posed for the statue.

The infantry warriors were surrounded by cavalry troops on horses, chariots, including the emperor's bronze replica, and were depicted carrying weapons such as swords, spears, and crossbows.

The pit housing the warriors was surrounded by other pits which, when excavated, housed terra cotta figures which reflected the everyday of the time of the emperor's death.

All of the figures had originally been painted, which had worn off over the centuries. It was a truly magnificent archaeological site, unlike any Harold had ever seen before.

The couple walked, did their Tai Chi exercises, and worked out every day. By the time they were slated to fly back to Beijing they were totally rested, and were ready to address the next phase of their lives.

They visited several sites in Beijing, including the Imperial Tombs of the Ming and Qing Dynasties exhibit located in the Northwest part of the city.

The cultural exhibit contained the burial tombs of thirteen of the sixteen Emperors of the time.

Akemi had completed, and sent her masters' thesis to the university in Tokyo, but had not heard if it had been approved as of yet. She had been told by her advisors that her work was superlative, and that in all probability, she would not have to defend her work in front of a committee.

Harold had a special treat in mind for her when she would hear the good news of her thesis acceptance and the completion of her degree.

Despite her belief that she would be informed quickly, Harold had his doubts, as he had remembered how his crossing of the finish line of his Doctoral degree had dragged on much longer than he had originally anticipated.

Her surprise could only be completed in warm weather, and at the point at which Harold's upcoming season, with whatever team signed him, would end.

Harold had done his own research on which major league teams would need a player like him, who could contribute in many ways, for the upcoming season.

He had talked with baseball people he respected about his chances for a contract, and what he should expect in terms of compensation if he was signed.

Gatewood knew he was ready to complete his comeback, based on his performance, the changes he had made in his game, and how he felt physically. He only needed major league baseball to agree with him.

"Hello, Harold. This is, Randle."

"Hi. How are you?"

"Thanks for asking Harold. I am doing fine."

"That's great. I have been thinking about you."

"Harold, I have been working hard for you."

"I always appreciate your efforts. Randle."

"Harold, I want to wish you and Akemi the best. Congratulations on your wedding."

"Thank you."

"Now maybe all of the rest of the world's most beautiful women can stop chasing you."

"That was funny, Randle."

"Your world's most eligible bachelor days are over Harold."

"I was more than ready for that."

"She must be quite a lady."

"Thank you. She is."

"I have news for you, some of which is good, and some of which is not."

"Okay. What is it? What are my options?"

"I talked to every team in the majors when I was in Nashville at the Winter baseball meetings."

"What did you find out?"

"There was some interest, but not at the major league level."

"From how many teams?"

"Three."

"Had they scouted me?"

"Yes, all three had done so in Central Illinois when you were with the Magicians, and also in Japan when you were with the Giants."

"What was verdict?"

"All three think you can make a comeback, but that you need another year."

"Well, that is good and bad news."

"They like your versatility, being able to play three positions."

"What about my hitting?"

"They like the fact that you have gone back to your original style, and think that you look better now than you have in years."

"What kind of off offer did they have in mind?"

"Start in the minors and prove yourself."

"I understand."

"There is one other thing. They want to see if your arm is good enough to catch eighty, to one, hundred, games a year."

"And if it is, what will they do?"

"If it is Harold, then those three and most of the rest of the teams will want to talk with you."

"Where would I start?"

"The low-level minors, A ball."

"What kind of contract?"

"Poor. They want you to play for almost nothing."

"How can they justify that?"

"I argued with them. Due to your injury history, and your age, they don't want to take on a big salary due to risks involved."

"I understand that."

"Harold, I don't think they are treating you right."

"I agree. But they are in charge of how they want to structure their rosters."

"Let me ask you something, Harold."

"Okay."

"Did you like playing in Japan?"

"Yes, I loved it there. But the problems were too severe to warrant dealing with the yakuza again."

"Yes, I think that the Giants gave you a raw deal when they released you. But, had you stayed, you would have been looking over your shoulder, fearing for your life."

"And that of my wife's also. Had I resigned with them, I was going to hire two more bodyguards in order to have around the clock protection."

"That is no way to live, Harold."
"I know."
"There is one other team in Japan which will sign you, Harold."
"Which one?"
"The Orman Pelicans."
"What plans would they have for me?"
"Platoon in left field."
"I don't think that would be good for my comeback."
"I agree."
"What kind of money?"
 "Less than half of what you made in Japan."
"That's no good, unless that is my only option."
"No. There are some other options."
"What are they?"
"First, in South Korea, with the Kiku Sycamores."
"What are their thoughts?"
"They want you to platoon at third base."
"What kind of money?"
"About sixty percent of what you earned in Japan."
"Who else is interested?"
"This one is not so hot Harold."
"The Taiwan Starlight League in Taiwan, China."
"Which team?"
"The Lagoon Dragons."
"What kind of money?"
"About twenty percent of what you made with the Giants."
"That is no good."
"Are there any other options?"
'Two."
"Who are they?"
"The Central Illinois Magicians, where you played at the start of the season this past year."
"Is Pat Sullivan still managing?"
"Yes."
"What do you think Scott?"
"The only way you should sign there is if you have no other offer. You've moved on past this level in your comeback."
"I agree."
"There is one more team which may be a good fit for you Harold. It is safe, away from the yakuza, would fit into your new life, and they are now offering about the same money as you made las year."

"Who is it?"

"The Beijing Tigers in the China Gold League."

"I have been to their stadium."

"Yes, somehow the pictures of you and Akemi that were in your wedding album were in the papers today?"

"What papers?"

"All of the major papers here in the United States. That is one reason I called you today."

"Hold on a minute, Scott."

"Akemi, please knock on the neighbor's door and see if we can look at their newspaper."

"Okay, Harold."

"Scott, what do the pictures look like?"

"You are both standing at home plate, with your arms around each other in one picture."

"And what else?"

"In the second one, she is sitting on your knee while you both are on the top steps of the Tigers' dugout."

"Are they embarrassing?"

"No, they are really cute. And, I think that they did you some good, because the Tigers called this morning and raised their offer."

"What are they offering?"

"The same amount as you made last year."

"What plans do they have for me?"

"They said you can play left field, some third and first base, and that you can catch some if you want."

"How many games can I catch?"

"As many as you want, as long as your arm holds up and you can produce."

"Hold on a minute Randle. Akemi is bringing me the paper."

"What do you think Harold?"

"Well, they are private pictures from the wedding. On the other hand, they are cute.

"Harold, what is the caption in the paper, about the pictures?"

"Here it is. Vice-President of China's daughter makes a catch."

"Oh, how great is that!"

"What did the paper in America write?"

"Is this American baseball player able to make a comeback? Harold Gatewood, with a nine-year career, has been out of the major leagues for three years. He has not been sitting by the fireplace acting like a retired person, as he has become a national hero in Spain, where he helped stop a terrorist attack, and where he helped the local police catch a serial killer."

"Oh, my. What else is in the story Randle?"

"It tells about how you helped save the president of Cuba's life, and how you helped stop a coup from overthrowing the government."

"Is there anything in there about Christina Abene?"

"Yes, they wrote about that."

"Is there anything else?"

"Yes, they talk about the troubles with the Giants, the Mafia Princess, the gambling and drug sales by the Yakuza, a player's suicide leap from a hotel, AIO terrorists, and how Akemi was almost killed, but was saved by her bodyguard."

"Oh no, there goes Akemi and my privacy over here."

"Are you both okay, Harold?"

"I think so. Akemi has her hand on my shoulder and has a big smile on her face so if she is ok, then things are fine."

"Harold, you may be a little upset with this story, and the pictures slipping out, but this may be a big boost for your career."

"How?"

"I think the Beijing Tigers see this as an opportunity to sign you, and have you be the face of the franchise."

"To use me as a publicity stunt?"

"No, they told me that they liked your history, and that Akemi and your romance is a wonderful story, one China will embrace.

Harold, the caliber of play is not as good as Japan, but it is a good option. If you produce, you will be scouted, which is what you want. And, you can catch when your arm is sound."

"Do you see any negatives Randle?"

"Not as long as you both are fine with it."

"I will talk to her about it."

"Call me back. I think I can get the Tigers to up their offer a little more. I will see if I can get you more than you were making in Tokyo last season."

"I will."

After Harold hung up the phone, Akemi smiled, laughed, looked at Harold, and asked him what he thought about the new events, the article, and the pictures.

They talked about the pros and cons of staying in Beijing to play for the Tigers, how it would impact their lives, how her parents might view the decision, and if Harold had another option which would be better for his career.

The stars seemed to be aligning to send a message that Harold should become a Beijing Tiger.

Akemi called her parents, to see if they had read the article, and if so, to get their thoughts on what the couple should do, and if it would create a problem for her father's career.

Her parents were overjoyed at the possibility the couple could stay in Beijing, and were not concerned about how it might impact their own lives.

Harold called Randle Quinn back and told him the couple was fine with the possibility of playing for the Tigers if the details of the overall plan and the compensation package were beneficial.

They would wait to hear how the outcome of Randall Quinn's conversation with the Beijing Tigers would unfold.

Chapter 10

Good News for the New Year

January 4

THE CHRISTMAS SEASON passed quickly, as the couple enjoyed their first holiday season as husband and wife.

As they all agreed, Harold's parents would hold the couple's presents until they returned to Illinois in the Fall, after the upcoming baseball season.

Harold had sent money to his parents in order that they could get what they wanted.

During the couple's recent trip to Illinois, he had found out what his parents wanted, and knew they would be able to enjoy it once the envelope and checks arrived.

Harold had thought about Christmas, and how his mom would have the house covered in Christmas decorations, and how his dad would have the outside of the house and the yard adorned in full Christmas tradition, with a nativity scene, snow men and Santa Claus statues, and many flashing outside lights.

New Year's Day in America had also passed quickly, as Harold was not one to celebrate the holiday, and Akemi's culture celebrated their own new year later in calendar year.

The bright side of the passing of the twelve days since Harold and his agent had spoken was that the time for nailing down a contract was soon approaching.

"Harold, Happy New Year... This is Randle Quinn."
"Happy New Year to you, Randle."
'Thanks."
"How are you, Randle?"
"I'm doing fine."
"What do you have for me?"
"Good news for the new year."
"What is it?"
"I made real progress for you. I was able to get several teams to bump up their offer substantially."

"How much?"

"The whole market went up, and we were able to use a bidding war to raise your contract offers by a million dollars a year."

"Which teams are still interested in me?"

"The Kiku Sycamores in South Korea and the Beijing Tigers in China."

"Which offer is best?"

"Financially, the Beijing Tigers are a bit higher."

"What perks did they include if any?"

"Both teams would provide you with a free apartment, and endorsement opportunities."

"That sounds fantastic. Did they provide the escape clause we asked for?"

"Yes, if they would move you to another team, you will be paid a bonus. If you use it to become a member of a major league team in America, you would be able to keep your current contract amount as a minimum, and negotiate any possible new contract amount with your new team."

"Great."

"What do you think Randle?"

"They won't go any higher, and there are no other teams in the running. This is the best you can do Harold, and it is a very good contract."

"Then I am going to be a Beijing Tiger."

"Great, Harold. They want to have you sign the contract at the ballpark tomorrow at one in the afternoon."

"I will be there."

"They will go over the contract with you."

"Is there anything I should look for in it, based on what we talked about today?"

"Just look it over. The items I mentioned will be in separate clauses, just like all of your other previous contracts. I will be in my office. Call me if you have any questions."

Harold, I would fly over there and be there myself but Claudia is still very sick, and in the hospital."

"I understand. Is there anything I can do for both of you?"

"Say a prayer for her."

"We will."

"Thanks, Harold. This is a good contract for you, and Akemi. You will be able to stay in China, and continue your comeback."

"I appreciate your help, Randle."

"You're welcome. Play like you can and you should be positioned to sign your next contract here in America."

"Thanks. We're getting close."

Harold walked over to Akemi, put his arm around her, kissed her and told her "We're going to be Beijing Tigers".

She was ecstatic, and smiled and giggled like a teenager.

The next day, Harold was picked up by a limousine the team had agreed to send for him.

As car pulled up to the front of the stadium, Harold looked at the glassed-in entrance, above which a red painted façade with Chinese symbols and words spelled out what he thought would be Hencheng Field, Home of the Tigers.

As Harold stepped out of the limo, he saw two mascots, Tigers in a green colored baseball uniform and cap, one on each side of the entrance doors.

Atop the entrance area were thirteen flagpoles, the center one displaying the red and yellow flag of the country of China.

He tipped his driver, thanked him for the ride, and walked through the entrance doors, into the stadium, and down to the area behind the screen behind home plate.

He surveyed the field, noticing the distances to each area of the outfield fence, and the hitting background for his future trips to the batter's box.

It was a nice stadium, one which he was going to call home.

He thought of his dad, of all the coaches and people who had helped him over his career, and his days of going to the Gibson City athletic field on his own to practice his throwing, footwork, and hitting skills.

He had come a long way from those days in Gibson City.

It had been a wonderful journey, one which he was not going to let end before he completed his return to the big leagues in America.

Beijing was now the current stop in that baseball safari.

Harold saw three men approaching him, turned, walked up the stairs toward them, stopped, bowed, and introduced himself. The men welcomed him, bowed, then introduced themselves as the President of the Beijing Tigers, the General Manager, and the man who would be his new Skipper, Hui Jun, whose name meant

"Wise ruler".

Harold hoped the translation would be true.

After a few moments of conversation, the four men went upstairs to the Tiger's office of the president, reviewed the contract details, and completed the signing ceremony.

Television crews from the Beijing newspapers were there to film the signing, and then to conduct interviews.

Besides the usual baseball-related questions, Harold was asked how he liked China, to which he replied that he loved the beauty of the country and was most appreciative of the acceptance the people had shown to he and his wife.

After the interview, and the completion of the signing ceremony, Harold made arrangements to start his future workouts at the stadium, then headed home to Akemi.

"Welcome home, Harold."

"Hi."

"Your interview was good. My best friend, my maid of honor, at our wedding, called and said she and her husband had already bought season tickets."

"Great. You'll have someone to go to the games with when we are playing at home."

"Yes, we talked about that."

"Do you think your parents will go to some of the games?"

"My mother might go with me, even though she doesn't like baseball, because it is too slow. My father is a big fan, but will have to have a security guard with him due to his political office."

"We get four tickets to all home games so you can bring them as often as you want."

"Harold, I talked to my father today."

"What did he say?"

"He said that he had taken the wedding pictures we gave them to his office to show his staff."

"Did they like the pictures?"

"He said that the two pictures which were in the papers were missing."

"Missing?"

"Yes. Who do you think took them?"

"I have no idea."

In one of the offices of the Zhongnanhai, the building and office location of the central government of China, a short, stout man, wearing light-colored framed glasses, and sporting thick black hair combed straight back on his head, had turned off the television at the conclusion of the interview.

He then had thrown the newspaper article which had announced that Harold Gatewood was scheduled to sign his contract with the Beijing Tigers that afternoon, to the floor in disgust.

"I had my mole in his office steal the two pictures from his desk, then I sent them to the newspapers to have them show the people of the country the disgrace of his family and his daughter for her act of marrying a foreigner.

He married a Japanese woman. Now his daughter has continued the disgraceful actions by not marrying a Chinese man.

The press is now making his daughter and son-in-law the darlings of the people of Beijing and the country.

He has always been my Achilles Heel. I will do everything in my power to bring him down, and take his place as Vice-President."

With those comments now filling the air, and his mind, Min Jun sat down in his chair and plotted his revenge for Guo Gang, Akemi's father.

Chapter 11

Settling Old Scores

January 6

MASARO HAYATO HAD walked up the sidewalk toward his parent's home with worried thoughts on his mind.

His father, Daisuke Hayato, had not been the same since Masaru's sister, Kimiko Hayato, former second-in-command at the Yamaguchi Gumi crime family, had met her death while trying to kill Mrs. Harold Gatewood, the former Akemi Gang His father's irrational hatred for Harold Gatewood, and his inability to end his grieving for Kimiko's death, had caused Daisuke to consider Hari – Kiri.

Masaru's mother had tried everything to pull her husband back from the precipice of suicide, and now, out of options, she had called her son to the home to help decide what could be done with Daisuke.

Upon entering the home, Masaru found the entry way into the main home in disarray, with books, papers, and an overturned end table on the floor.

Afraid that there might be intruders in the home, and fearing the worst for his parents, Masaru drew his pistol from its holster, and proceeded, step by step, into the kitchen, where disarray was also present.

Slowly, and carefully, Masaru rounded the corner of the living room, his pistol at the ready.

Masaru's fears were materialized when he saw his mother laying on her side, with a pool of blood on the carpet near her head.

Near her, he saw his father laying on his back, with his prized ceremonial Hari – Kiri sword buried in his stomach.

Both were dead, for how long Masaru was unsure. He looked at his parents, then walked to the nearest chair, sat down, buried his head in his hands, and wept like a baby.

As a member of the inner circle of the Yamaguchi Gumi crime family, Masaru was used to violence and death.

But, first his sister's death, and now both of his parent's brutal deaths, which he knew was the result of another crime family trying to wrestle power from his organization, had hit him hard, causing his grief to overwhelm him.

After regaining his composure, Masaru thought about what he should do.

First, for his own safety, he should make sure the home was secure, and free of those who had killed his parents.

Next, he should call the police in order that they could take the required normal actions in situations like this one.

Finally, he should call his crime family lieutenants to the office, assess the damage to the crime family, and plan his revenge.

The probable opposing crime family which had killed his parents, and was challenging the Yamaguchi Gumi's hold on the total Yakuza organization was the Sukiyaki Kai.

After addressing the crime family's business, he would then turn to revenge on his personal family's nemesis, Harold Gatewood.

After the police, and the coroner, had completed their processing of the murder scene, Masaru headed to the crime family office to meet his lieutenants to discuss current business and the day's tragedy.

"Gentlemen, thank you for coming. As you now know the head of the Yamaguchi Guich family were murdered today."

"We are sorry to lose our leader. And we are sorry for your personal loss of your parents."

"Thank you. We will address our plans to avenge those losses after we conduct our business meeting."

"Yes sir."

"Gentlemen, let's review the monthly numbers."

"Yes, sir."

"Let's look at recruitment. How many new members did we add this month?"

"Three-thousand-five-hundred, twenty-eight. Our total staff is now one-hundred-five-thousand, six-hundred-forty-three, loyal members."

"That is very good growth. By how much did we exceed our goal?"

"We had four-hundred, and six, members more than we projected."

"Excellent."

"What was the increase in the area of cyber-crime? """

"Eighty-four percent."

"Good. Is there still room for growth in this new area?"

"Yes."

"Continue to press the members for more revenue in this area."

"Yes, sir."

"What took place in the drug segment?"

"Up eleven percent, sir."

"It is a stable market but we still have room for growth."

"Yes. This segment is a cash cow for our operation."

"What about the sex trade figures?"
"Again, they were up, with new outlets, and higher demand."
"By how much?"
"Thirty percent."
"Excellent."
"What about the human trafficking segment?"
"Up eleven percent."
"That is also good."
"How did our money-laundering operation perform?"
"Up eight percent."
"We can do better this year. Put pressure on all of the members in this area for more results."
"Yes, sir."
"Why do you think this area was down?"
"We needed to shore up our money laundering operation in the United States. This will allow us to move more drugs through Hawaii into the United States, and then firearms back through Hawaii and into Japan."
"Good. Follow up on those actions and let me know of the progress monthly."
"Yes, sir."
"What about the extortion figures?"
"Up nine percent."
"We can do better. Concentrate on government figures and politicians we can blackmail through use of our stable of girls."
"Yes sir. The politicians are always a good source of prospects for this area."
"We talked about weapon sales as it related to money laundering.
"Do you have anything to add about weapon sales?"
"No. We have covered that in detail."
"What about the solidity of our front businesses?"
"They are stable. We can always add a restaurant or another cash business if we need to."
"What about our gambling division?"
"All areas of that segment are doing fine except one."
"What area is that?"
"Probable online and bookie bets on the professional baseball was dismal last year due to the many problems, and because of Harold Gatewood."
"We will get to the Harold Gatewood problem in a minute. How do you plan to turn that around?"
"I think we need to buy a second skybox at the stadium for the Yomiuri Giants games here in Tokyo.

We need to bring in more high rollers, develop an interest in the team, and try to get an insider to feed us information on current injuries, and events which would impact the betting odds.

We should be able to find a front office person who needs some extra money."

"Do you think the problems of last year can be overcome?"

"Yes, sir. People will always bet on baseball."

"Okay. That is a good plan. Have you identified any possible people we can target?"

"No, not as of yet."

"What kind of team will they have this year?"

"They will content for the title again, despite getting rid of Gatewood. They still need some pitching depth and a good utility player to help out at several positions."

"Implement the proposed actions. Do they have American players again?"

"Yes. Two at a time, per year."

"Some Americans are very greedy, with no honor. They may be easy to bribe. As always, ingratiate yourself with the team, and see if any of them can be used for our purposes."

"Yes, sir."

"Do you have anything else to report, Gentlemen?"

"No, sir."

"You are doing very well in your positions. We are at a dangerous point where other families are trying to wrestle power from us. Be very careful, and stay the course."

"Yes, sir."

"Are there any questions anyone?"

"Yes, sir. I have a general one."

"Go ahead."

"Other than our regular business duties, what will we be doing in the next few weeks?"

"Settling old scores."

"I understand, sir."

"Gentlemen, every few years the Sumiyoshi Kai family tries to take over part of our territory, our income stream, our membership, segments of our organization, and control of the entire Yakuza family."

"Yes, sir, we have been through the wars with them."

"It is again time to send them a message. This time, it will be especially strong for what they did to my father and mother."

"We all agree and look forward to the mission."

"I want you to pick three of our best men in the Revenge and Enforcement Division for a special mission."

"Yes, sir. Should they require any special skills?"

"Other than the usual killing skills, they should have a special enjoyment for blood lust, and brutality."

"Yes, sir."

"The mission will require the three men to monitor the residence of the head of the Sumiyoshi Kai crime family, enter it, and use baseball bats to beat the man into the start of his death journey."

"Are there any other special instructions?"

"The murder should be especially brutal. It should send a message to them for what they did, and it should also emphasize that the murder will be the first of many if they continue to try to take control of our operation."

"When do you want it done, sir?"

"Start on it immediately, after the meeting."

"I understand."

"That leads us to another matter which needs to be settled on a permanent basis."

"Harold Gatewood?"

"Yes, Mr. Harold Gatewood. He has caused us more than enough aggravation."

"We all agree."

"Who is or very best assassin?"

"For what type of work?"

"He or she should be especially qualified for a revenge killing, in response for the death of my sister, and my parents."

"What type of skills will be needed?"

"The mission will require the ability to blend in, monitor and survey the target, remain unnoticed, and carry out an extremely painful and agonizing death for the target."

"Sir, what will be the location of the assignment?"

"I read in the morning paper where Harold Gatewood just signed to play baseball with the Beijing Tigers in China. That will be the location."

"China? It will be difficult for our man to gain entry and remain unnoticed since our country is having trouble with China's expansion actions in the South and East China Seas."

"Yes, that is correct. And, it is why our man must be able to blend in once he gets to China."

"Sir, are there any contacts we can use inside China to help our operative move about China freely?"

"We can possibly pay the Tongs for help. And, there is one other possibility. I am exploring the second option at this time."

Gentlemen, who do you recommend for this very Important assignment?"

"I think the man for the job is Isamu Goro."

"Are there any other recommendations?"

"Sir, I think we all feel he is our most reliable, and the deadliest killer we have."

"I know that he was shot during his last assignment. What is the status of his health at this time?"

"He has fully recovered."

"What is his mental condition at this time?"

"Sir, do you mean his mental ability to bounce back from being shot?"

"Yes, give me that one first, please."

"He has recovered psychologically from the shooting."

"What about his general psychiatric make up?"

"Sir, he is a sociopath. He is extremely brutal in his killing assignments, preferring to slowly torture his victims before eliminating them."

"Very good. What are his specialties?"

"Long range marksmanship, hand to hand combat, use of poisons and mind-altering drugs, torture techniques, victim mutilation, mental mind games, and pure sadistic killing for the sheer pleasure of it."

"What kind of targets has he eliminated?"

"Men, women, children, old, young, rich, poor, it makes no difference to him as long as he can kill them in the manner he likes."

"He sounds like our man."

"He is a real jewel when it comes to killing, sir."

"Gentlemen. Let's vote on it. Is he our choice to take care of Harold Gatewood?"

The vote was a resounding yes.

"Good. Start preparing him for the mission immediately."

"Consider it done. sir. We all want Gatewood to suffer a horrible death."

Chapter 12

"This Time"

January 6

IT HAD BEEN a familiar yet disappointing scene. Eight men, patriots at heart, said their helloes, then took their appropriate seats at a large rectangular-shaped table.

On the wall above the chair at the far end of the table was the red, green and white flag of the Basque people. The tall, black-haired mustachioed man rose from his chair and spoke.

"Welcome fellow freedom fighters. Long Live the Basque people."

"Welcome! We salute you."

"Scribe, please note the presence of the five Regional Commanders, their Assistant Regional Commanders, the Assistant National Commander, and, myself, Ekain Koldo, the National Commander."

"Completed, sir."

"With our attended members, all three areas of our AIO organization are represented. Those areas are our Logistics, Political, and Military divisions."

Nods of the twelve heads acknowledged each of the division representatives.

Tonight, we continue our long struggle for self-determination, establishment of our country borders, the free use of our language, and the enjoyment of our proud culture.

May we always be free, never again to suffer the indignities forced upon us by the dictator Franco."

Ten pairs of hands pounded the table in approval of the National Commander's comments."

"Our meeting tonight will include reports from all divisions, and the vote on a proposed operation. Would the Regional Commander in charge of membership please read his report?"

"Sir, the membership numbers have declined by nineteen percent, due largely to the dissatisfaction with the results of the failure of Operation Ice Chest and the death of our comrades during the San Fermin Murder spree by our operative Zigor Kerbasi, and the failure of our agents in Cuba, and in Tokyo, to eliminate our nemesis, Harold Gatewood.

The results could have been worse had it not been for poor economic conditions in Spain, which still allows us to recruit new members who are faced with dismal job prospects.

The downturn in membership is in the younger age group, which is demanding that retaliatory action be taken against Harold Gatewood, whom they consider, as we all do, a symbol of our failure to successfully advance our mission for Basque independence."

"I understand Are there any questions or comments?"

"No, sir."

"We will discuss Mr. Gatewood after our reports have been given."

"Fine."

"What is the financial report?"

"Sir, the finances are still down, eleven percent, due to losses in our membership dues and our poor results in the revenue producing areas."

"Thank you. Any questions?"

"No."

Can we please now, from our Regional Commander of the Political Division, hear the developments in that area?"

"Sir, the bad news is that our efforts in the political arena have additional shown backward movement."

"What are the causes?"

"The world community still continues to label the AIO a terrorist organization due to our use of violence, and the failed missions in the recent past as previously mentioned.

Also, we have suffered terrible criticism related to the attempts to kill Harold Gatewood here in Spain, Cuba, and in Tokyo."

"I understand the backlash and we will discuss that later.

We were aware that criticism would come when we moved in that direction."

"Sir, we tried a political approach, a more peaceful outreach, when we offered a cease fire of our military actions."

"Yes, and that olive branch was rejected."

" Yes, sir. We also offered to disband our organization if we could be granted independence and our goal of self-determination in the areas our people have lived in for centuries."

"Correct. Unfortunately, that offer was flatly rejected."

"That is correct."

"What is the progress report in the area in of prisoner's rights?"

"Sir, we have lobbied for better conditions, the end of torture, and a plea to not house our patriots in prisons which are far spread out from each other."

"What has been the result of those efforts?"

"Sir, all have failed."

"What else can you report?"

"Sir, the gains through the use of political efforts are often reversed when elections result in the change of political leadership, and ideologies."

"Thank you. Does anyone have any input or questions?"

"No, sir."

"Would the Regional Commander handling the military arm of our organization please give us his report?"

"Sir, our organization is now more organized than in the past. Based on feedback from our membership, the opinion is that the military division is the preferred segment of our organization."

"We needed to be more organized in our actions toward Gatewood but I am glad the membership still wants action. Go on please."

"All of the regions have asked for more military training."

"We have beefed up our training for our field operatives after the recent failures. Please continue."

"The membership favors more aggressive tactics and action now."

"That is very encouraging, Commander."

"Sir, violence may be our best approach to turn around our membership and financial troubles."

"Thank you. Any comments or questions?"

None were aired.

"Thank you for your reports. Our next agenda item is a discussion, consideration of, and vote on a possible military style action on a well-known target, one who deserves, and needs to be, eliminated.

In front of you, on the overhead screen, you will see the details of the news which some of you may have seen recently.

Mr. Harold Gatewood is again back in baseball, ad has just signed with the Beijing Tigers in China to join their organization. He has been living in Beijing with his new wife, the daughter of the Vice-President of China.

An aggressive, violent approach, the type of which our members are wanting, is definitely in Mr. Gatewood's future. Any comments anyone?"

"Yes, sir. We have failed numerous times before. Our membership is demanding that we must succeed."

"Comrades, this time, we will succeed. This operation would give us an opportunity to go back to more terrorist acts which would highlight our goals.

These types of actions create fear and panic, and have been proven to be successful in bringing us quicker positive results."

The faces of the twelve men were marked with concern, their eyes locked on the details of the news about their foil, now living in Beijing.

Harold Gatewood had caused many problems for the AIO, the results of which had made their lives miserable over the last two years. It was a continuing boil which refused to quit festering.

"The question to be decided is if this military action, called Operation Tiger Slayer, should be implemented."

Discussion on the pros and cons of the organization's increased use of more violent actions, and the approval or rejection of the plan, went on for a few tense minutes. The vote was taken, and the result was announced.

"My Friends, the operation is approved by unanimous vote. The Assistant National Commander and I would like to now address the assignment of the operative to be assigned to the mission, and discuss the strategy and tactics required to successfully accomplish our task."

"Yes. sir. We all agree. Let's proceed."

"What is the current status of our field agent agents?"

"Sir, we have suffered a reduction in our field operative area due to the deaths of Autor Lehoi and Gabriel Domeka, when Mr. Gatewood led the CIO and the local police authorities to the Lehoi estate in an arrest mission."

"Yes. We still owe him a painful lesson for that action."

"We also lost Andoni Mikola when he tried to kill Gatewood at the airport."

"Yes, he was a rising star in our organization who will be missed. We need to settle the score with Mr. Gatewood on that matter also."

"We all agree that Gatewood must die."

"He has been a thorn in our side for too long."

"We also lost one of our best field agents when Bakar Kemen was killed at the Havana airport while attempting to eliminate Gatewood before he and his finance Christina Abene left the country."

"Yes, that was another embarrassment."

"We also lost his brother Bittor Kemen in Tokyo when he was thrown off the rooftop by the CIO agent assigned to protect Gatewood.

"Yes, that is also correct. The mission may be complicated by several factors related to the location in Beijing. We may not have an agent who can function in that environment."

"We may have a person who can help with those details."

"Who?"

"Our man we had on the payroll in Havana, and Tokyo, and who helped both of the Kemen bothers in many ways."

"Do you mean Roger Caldwell?"

"Yes."

"How can he help if he is in Tokyo?"

"He isn't. He is now with the American Embassy in Beijing."

"Great. Will be still cooperating with us?"

"He has not changed. He is still very greedy. If we throw enough money at him again, I am sure he will help us in Beijing."

"Can we afford him again?"

"Yes. And, we need to get Gatewood. The money will be well spent again, and aid us in our mission."

"Good point."

"Comrades, our goal, our strategy, would be to infiltrate China, set up operations in Beijing, and eliminate Gatewood.

We also would need to get our operative out of the country after the killing."

"It will be an ambitious plan, as you mentioned."

"What suggestions do you have?"

"Besides Roger Caldwell, who else can be of help?"

"We have no other contacts in China who could help. We are going to need to rely heavily on Roger Caldwell."

"What about the Chinese government? Gatewood's wife is the Vice-President's daughter."

"That may create some leverage for us."

"Sir, does her father have any political enemies?"

"Her father is a strong, well-liked politician. But he should have enemies we can use to our benefit."

"What about the Tong criminal element in China?"

"That might be a good option also."

"Perhaps we should plan on doing the mission ourselves. If we can get any help from other sources that would be a nice plus.

Maybe we can get logistical help from Roger Caldwell's connections."

"Very well, Comrades. Who do we have that is capable, and can handle the mission?"

"I have the ideal candidate. He has been through all of our training, excelling in all phases of the program."

"Has he been in the field before?"

"Yes. He performed a series of political blackmailing missions against five politicians in the Spanish government who would not pay us to keep their affairs with married woman confidential."

"He is not averse to killing?"

"No. He rather enjoys it. He has a criminal record, with three kills in civilian life, and two for us in the line of duty."

"In the line of duty?"

"Yes sir, official kills. He also had an affair with a female North Korean agent, and ended up killing her in an accidental affixation during a sex act."

Was it really an accident?"

"It is hard to say, sir. He claimed it was an accident, but then he smiled and laughed."

"Comrades, we need someone fearless, and not afraid to do whatever is needed."

"I am confident he would qualify on all counts."

"Is he loyal?"

"Yes, he comes from a family which has been loyal to our cause for many years. The family has sent two relatives to contribute as field operatives.

He believes in the AIO goal of self-determination and independence and wants to contribute in any way he can."

"Excellent."

"He also brings a desire for revenge against Mr. Gatewood."

Why?"

"Sir, his cousins were Bakar and Bittor Kemen, who were assigned to eliminate the American when he was in Cuba, and Tokyo."

"He sounds like a man with the blood lust we need for this mission. Who is he?"

"Eneko Itzal."

"What kind of name is that?"

"It is Basque of course. And, it means 'my shadow', a perfect man for an assassin who must tail his victims.".

"He sounds like the man we need to settle the score for us with Harold Gatewood. It there are no comments or concerns, we should vote on his assignment to Operation Tiger Slayer."

The vote was unanimous in favor of the assignment. Eneko Itzal was now the hope of the AIO to fulfill its desire to be done with Gatewood forever.

For Itzal, it was a chance to avenge his two cousins' deaths. He would soon leave for Beijing, to meet his destiny.

His instructions were to kill Gatewood, or not return alive.

Chapter 13

Retirement

January 7

HE HAD MADE the trip many times, but today would be a final journey packed with good and bad news.

As he headed toward the corner office of the building, Deputy CIO Director Rick Owens was still sleepy, after a late arrival from his annual ski trip to Colorado.

He loved Aspen, and the slopes of Beaver Creek, as it was the one place, he could escape the pressures of his job.

He had been off for ten days, and had not missed the office, not even a little bit.

Owens longed for the time when he could retire, ridding himself of national and international problems, and living like a normal human being away from the spotlight of politics.

Inside the office, CIO Director Carlton Chase was sitting behind his desk, stirring a cup of coffee with cream and sugar, and gazing at a piece of paper which evidently was of little importance, based on the relaxed expression on his face, and the fact that today was his last day of work before his retirement.

He had spent eighteen years in the position, longer than any CIO Director in the agency's history.

Chase had served good presidents, and bad, always done so with dignity and true professionalism.

He looked forward to retirement in the Florida Keys where he could fish for bonefish, snook, and tarpon in the backwaters off Islamorada, and for marlin, dorado, and tuna in the Atlantic Ocean.

Chase's dream would only be interrupted by a month of hunting pheasant, grouse, and partridge in Idaho.

He had served his country, and soon he would be leaving the office for the last time.

"Hello Rick. Welcome back."

"Thanks."

"How was your trip?"

"It was great. The slopes were filled with white powder, and the skiing was wonderful."

"Did you have any problems?"

"Not on the slopes. The road back to the airport was packed with weekend skiers as always."

It is good to have you back, even though you may want to still be on vacation."

"Thank you, Carlton."

"As you can see, I have our new Deputy Director, Terry Robbins, with me. "

"Congratulations, Terry. You are the man for the job.

"Thank you, Director Chase."

"Soon, you will have the pleasure of reporting to Rick once he takes his new position as director"

"Yes, sir. I am looking forward to it."

"Rick, I have been waiting for a long time to say this next comment. Do you have the last incident report you and I will ever go over?"

"That's funny, Carlton."

"Let's take a look at it."

"Yes, sir."

"Hopefully we can get some good news this morning."

"I hope so."

"Let's start with South America."

"Okay. The good news is that this region has seen no deterioration in conditions since our last report."

"That is good news. If only the rest of the world could follow suit."

"Yes, sir. Would you like to hear about Central America?"

"Yes."

"The situation is still getting worse. The illegal immigrant trade is still in full swing, with a flow of people from Central America coming through Mexico, and across the southern border and into the United States."

"We need to enforce border security."

"I agree. Congress needs to stop the flood of illegals. Border security can't keep up with the constant influx of people."

Owens then stated, "We have no way of knowing who these people are, and of vetting their background."

"One more year, and perhaps a new administration can implement a sensible program."

"That would be nice. It must be done or we are going to be hit with more terrorist attacks."

"What about the situation in Cuba, Rick?"

"Good news here, sir. The Bertalina government has stabilized since the coup attempt, and has a grip on any more possible takeover attempts."

"What about the embassy, and its effectiveness, in Havana?"

"It has done well. A new man has taken the reins there and relations look good so far. Investors are pouring money into the country and their economy looks like it will improve."

"Excellent, Rick."

"Thanks. Would you like to hear about the Middle East and their problems?"

"No, but if I must, please go ahead."

"The migration continues, as people still are fleeing to Europe."

"Have they slowed the pace into Greece?"

"Yes, sir, they can't cross the Aegean Sea due to the cold weather."

"That is a blessing. Many people died in the warm months on the boat trips."

"Yes, around five, thousand. people a day were taking the sea route to Greece."

"The migration is the results of the failed Arab Spring, and the removal of the leadership, Muammar Gaddafi of Libya."

"Yes. No thought was given to the follow up consequences of those actions."

"Yes, hundreds of thousands of people are on the move, uprooted by the seeds of events which have caused these actions."

"The administration has hinted that we in America might take over two hundred thousand refuges."

"I know. We can't possibly screen that many people properly, as we do not have the needed information about their backgrounds."

"Yes, we will suffer terrorists' attacks from this recklessness."

"Sir, the situation in Iraq is next."

"What is the report, Rick?"

"It continues to be a quagmire."

"The administration considered moving troops closer to the battlefield last Fall, and has gone back and forth on the issue, with what seems like no clear policy."

"Yes. The situation appears the same as before, with no clear path to leave the country."

"It is the same in Afghanistan. The current administration backed off their pledge last May to leave the country. Last fall, they announced they would keep advisory forces there until 2017."

"I know, sir."

"Terry, you will no doubt have to follow up on these never-ending problems with Rick in the future so please feel free to give us your input."

"I will, sir."

"Carlton, the next area concerns Iran and the nuclear arms treaty."

"What is new?"

"The pact was passed with all Democrat votes, and no votes from the Republicans. The Iranians have still continued to increase the processing of uranium, and are continuing to be very vocal against America and Israel."

"The joy of dealing with Iran is amazing. We made a bad mistake with that treaty."

"Sir, the last area is Syria."

"Okay."

"Russia entered the area last Fall to support the Bashar al-Assad regime. While it has caused concern and embarrassment for the administration, luckily no event has led to an international incident in the area so far."

"Thank goodness we were fortunate that Russia did not retaliate against Turkey for the shooting down of their jets, and the killing of their pilot."

"Yes, sir, the area is a powder keg."

"Terry, we talk freely in these incident meetings. Nothing we say goes beyond these walls."

"I understand, sir."

Owens continued, "Sir. the situation in Europe is still in confusion over the over the refuge migration into the area, with some countries taking in some of them, and some countries refusing to do so."

"That will have to play itself out as time goes on. But I think we are seeing the death of European culture due to their actions."

"The next area in the report concerns China."

"Please go ahead."

"The Chinese are still dumping their holdings of American dollars, and continue to push for the end of the dollar as the world currency standard.

They have tried to help their exports with a devaluation of the yuan, also called the renminbi."

"The currency wars continue to go on, Rick."

"Also, the disagreement with the Japanese over the Senkaku Islands continues.

It is based on historical differences over possible oil reserves, fishing rights, shipping and trading lanes, and hard feelings over Japan's invasion of the China in World War II."

"What is the recent historical background?"

"The islands are in the East China Sea. There are five uninhabited islands and three large rocky areas. The problems go back over many years.

In 2013 China initiated a no-fly, zone over the area, which has led to several incidents. China has also increased their own number of flights to monitor island air space. No military action has yet taken place.'

"Go on, Rick."

"The Chinese - Japanese relationship has always been complicated. Where does the United States stand in this situation?"

"Sir, by treaty, we are required to support Japan against Chinese aggression."

"Are there more issues in the area related to this situation?"

"Yes. China and Japan have also quarreled over the Korean situation in the area."

"Please review that situation for me."

"South Korea and Japan are our allies and we must support both countries against aggression by China or North Korea."

"Oh, yes, our buddy in North Korea. What is he up to?"

"He is fairly quiet right now, sir."

"We have to support Japan and South Korea. What is China's stance on this matter?"

"They understand the treaty agreements. They also control North Korea to some degree. The disagreements center in how much influence China should place on North Korea when it comes to Japanese and South Korean issues."

"We have the second and third largest economies in the world constantly at odds."

"It is always a balancing act, Carlton."

"What else, as it relates to China or Japan?"

"The Japanese crime family Yakuza, in particular the Yamaguchi Gumi branch in Tokyo, is still actively laundering money through the United States."

"How?"

"Drugs are sent through Hawaii into Chicago, Illinois, then the money from those sales are used to buy firearms which are shipped back through Hawaii to Japan, where they are sold."

"How big problem is it?"

"Massive, and it is growing."

"See what can be done about squashing it."

"Rick, have we had problems with the Yakuza before?"

"Yes. They are the second biggest crime family in the world."

"Please refresh my memory about them."

"The one family we need to monitor was headed by Daisuke Hayato."

"What is he like?"

"Was?"

"Yes 'was'."

"Is he dead?"

"Yes. He, and his wife, were killed. They were probably murdered by their rival crime family, the Sumiyoski Kai. He was as ruthless as a person can be."

"He had a daughter, correct?"

"Yes, Kimiko Michi Hayato, who was the second in command and the heir apparent to run the family, and all of the Yakuza organization.

She was intelligent, cunning, possibly more ruthless than her father, and a stone-cold dangerous killer."

"And, she was killed by the body guard of the daughter of the Vice President of China, correct?"

"Yes, sir. Kimiko was jealous of her ex-boyfriend falling in love with the daughter of the Chinese Vice President, Akemi Gang, who was born from a marriage of a Japanese mother and Chinese father."

"Who was the boyfriend, Rick?"

"You remember Sir. It was Harold Gatewood."

"Oh, yes, our buddy Harold Gatewood. I knew I could not get away from him, even on my last day in office."

"He and Akemi Gang are now married, and living in Beijing, China."

"In China?"

"Yes. He just signed to play baseball with the Beijing Tigers."

"How will the problems in Japan with the Yakuza be impacted by Gatewood and his wife's relationship with her father, the Vice President?"

"We don't know, but there could be problems if the new head of the Yamaguchi Gumi family, the son, Masaru Hayato, takes revenge on the Sumiyoski Kai crime family for killing his parents, and for trying to move in on his family's operation."

"Then what might happen, Rick?"

"Then, Masaru Hayato might try to eliminate Harold Gatewood, and maybe even his wife, for being the reason his sister was killed by the bodyguard of Gatewood's now wife, Akemi Gang, the daughter of the Vice President of China, Guo Gang."

"That action would possibly lead to an international incident between China and Japan, who are already at odds which each other for the reasons we discussed."

"Yes, sir."

"Rick, even on my last day on the job, I am haunted by Harold Gatewood. When I retire, I hope he does not show up on my doorstep in Islamorada."

"I understand. Your efforts have helped save his life more than once, but he has been a source of aggravation for you."

"He is a good, honorable man, but I will be glad not to deal with him on foreign matters again."

"I know. But, be assured he does appreciate all you have done for him."

"I am sure he does. Rick, please move on."

"The election of the coming year is the big news. The economy is still being touted as being great, but the public is not buying that line.

Terrorism is still a big fear. Illegal immigration and its' possible impact on people's safety is perhaps the number one issue."

"We spoke about the continuing immigration problem on the southern border. What is happening in Texas?"

"Texas announced last fall that sanctuary cities will not be tolerated in the state, and they are sticking to that comment."

"Good for Texas. Is there anything else domestically?"

"Not really. Things are quiet today."

"What about the AIO terrorist organization in Spain?"

"They appear to be somewhat quiet, as nothing has been heard from them since their agent Bittor Kemen was killed in Tokyo, when he was after Harold Gatewood."

"Do you think they have given up on setting the score with Mr. Gatewood?"

"I doubt it. He has put several embarrassing events at their doorstep, first in San Toro de Lidia, Spain, then in Havana, Cuba, and then in Tokyo, Japan. I think they will hound him until his dying day."

"I feel sorry for him, Rick. He has done some very honorable things, and he continues to be the target of a terrorist organization."

"Yes, sir. His life has been a series of highs and lows over the last three years. I think he may be a target again, as the AIO now knows where he is living in China."

"He would be safer if he stayed in the United States. The AIO organization is weak here."

"I agree."

"He is still on the comeback trail to the major leagues. I hope he makes it."

"So do I, Carlton."

"What about the embassy position in Beijing, China?'

"The embassy position has been filled."

"Who has the job?"

"Roger Caldwell."

"He was at the Havana, Cuba Embassy, then Tokyo, and is now in Beijing."

"Yes. He sounds like a good man."

"Is there anything else, Rick?"

"No."

"Rick, you have always done good work, and you always have supported me, which I have appreciated."

"Thank you. You have had a great career, Carlton."

"Thanks. I am happy that I recommended you to be the new CIO Director, Rick."

"Thank you."

"Keep doing a good job, and keep your nose clean, Rick. You know how this game is played. You will make a fine CIO Director."

"Thank you."

"Terry, you will be working with the best man for the job. I wish you well."

"Thank you, sir."

"Let's go to the retirement celebration guys. I want a big, delicious piece of chocolate cake."

"Lead the way, Carlton."

Chapter 14

Getting Ready

April 2

THE WINTER MONTHS in Beijing were cold, and Harold wished they were in the Florida Keys, or Panama, fishing for marlin, dorado, and tuna.

Akemi, despite enjoying being near her parents and her best friend in Beijing, also wanted to be somewhere warm, and be fishing with her husband.

After Harold's playing days, they would consider moving to a warm climate, or spending the winter months as a snowbird.

The couple had made new friends, enjoying mutual interests, and their individual interests as well.

Akemi had developed an interest in helping rape victims in Beijing, as the crime had become more widespread, especially during the warm, Summer and Fall months of the year.

She had gone to worked as an analyst at the country's national rape center, accumulating and analyzing data on the act, the victims, and in developing a national data base.

Harold had embarked on a very ambitious training schedule for the upcoming season, one even more concentrated than his usual dedicated regime.

He knew that this was his make-or-break season in terms of successfully returning to the major leagues.

He also knew that he had to return to his natural position, a catcher, for at least half of his playing time.

But he would continue to play left field, and first or third base, in a pinch, when he was not catching.

Catching was demanding, compared to playing the outfield, where he often felt he should be buying a ticket to watch the game.

As he stood in the outfield grass his mind would sometimes wander as he tried to come to grips with why he was not catching.

This year, he would make a return to at least part time play behind the plate, and see if his arm could stand up to the grind.

In addition to his isometric program, were the joint angle and muscle length during an exercise did not change, Harold increased his isotonic program.

He didn't like weight training, and had always been discouraged by Ernie White not to overdo it, he had decided that he needed to strengthen his leg muscles in preparation for the rigors catching.

He also incorporated more running exercises to build up his stamina.

Despite the obvious improvement in tone and strength, the running program had caused a weight loss.

Although he had always eaten sensibly, Harold had needed to increase his daily caloric intake, and had adjusted his eating habits to take in more fuel for his body.

The chore was a pleasant one, as Akemi was a great cook, and was able to easily provide what Harold's nutritionist had outlined.

Harold's arm had held up well in spring training, as he had insisted using his own throwing schedule, limiting his throws much the same way a pitcher limited his pitch count when coming back from Tommy John arm surgery.

He also refused to take infield practice before a game. Instead, he worked on his throwing footwork, without actually throwing, in the batting cage below the field, much the same as he had done as a boy at the athletic field in Gibson City.

Harold liked all of his teammates, and had spent three months working out with them at the stadium before the season 's opening day. They were professional, dedicated ballplayers, who respected each other.

Harold had been instrumental in bringing two other foreign players to Beijing Tigers.

He had known Kent Freeman, a third baseman, from his playing days in the United States.

He was a very good player, with strong skills in the five areas, running, throwing, fielding, hitting, and hitting for power. which were used to rank players by ability.

Kent was also a good competitor, one who would always hustle and try to win.

Harold had also urged the Tigers to sign his former Giant teammate, and roommate, Scott Binder. Scott was a durable, reliable pitcher, with good stuff, and a desire to win.

He had pitched well in Japan, and was slated to be a quality addition to the Tigers rotation.

He could start, or relieve, and would be used in both areas until his place in pitching puzzle could be solidified.

His Chinese teammates were molded in the traditional Asian manner, and would be good contributors to the team's success.

The style of play would be similar to that of last season's experience in Japan, a style in which Harold fit nicely.

They were all professionals with the typical range of personality quirks found on most baseball teams.

Only one player, Jing Heng, the All Star first basemen and league homerun champion, seemed to be an outlier in the normal distribution range of player personality.

For some reason, Heng was distant, sometimes surly, and always unpredictable. He could be very quiet, then suddenly explode in anger, at his teammates, or himself.

Harold sensed he was jealous of anyone who might steal the spotlight from him, and knew that playing a long season with him would be a trying experience for everyone.

When Heng was going well, he was fine, but when things did not go as planned, he could be very difficult.

The Chinese players gave him a wide berth, letting him go his own way at all times. He could go days without speaking to anyone, and was not known for heaping lavish praise on anyone, preferring to only to praise himself.

Jing Heng did want to be God, but he was sure that God wanted to be Jing Heng.

Only one event seemed to stir his soul, and bring a trance like smile to his face, hitting a homerun.

For this quality, Harold had nicknamed him "Home Run Heng", a title which no one dared repeat for fear of being verbally attacked. Harold had known many characters in his years in baseball, but this guy was a head case of the highest magnitude, and in a league of his own.

His off, field whereabouts and life were unknowns, as he would vanish like an apparition once he left the locker room.

The Beijing Tigers played in Division One of the China Baseball League, which had six teams, the Sichuan Dragons, the Tianjin Lions, the Guangdong Leopards, the Jianjin Pegasus, and the Shanghai Golden Eagles.

Division Two of the league had four teams, the Henan Elephants, the Shandong Institute of Commerce and Technology Baseball Club, the China Society baseball Club, and the People's Liberation Army Baseball Club.

The Tigers would be competitive, and hoped to win their division, and then the championship.

Chinese baseball, bangqiu, had wanted the Tigers to sign Harold for many reasons.

They had hoped his talent and leadership would help bring this year's championship to Beijing, that Harold would be the star the country and the league needed to capture the interest of the fans, and that he would serve as a role model for the game.

In addition, the fact that he had married the beautiful daughter of the country's Vice-President, and also that the country had viewed Harold and Akemi's wedding as an event on par with the marriage of Prince William and Prince Kate in the country of England, he had unwillingly become the face of Chinese baseball.

After Harold had announced his decision to sign with the Tigers, American Major League Baseball had contacted him to see if he would be willing to serve as the Ambassador of their fourth development center, located in Beijing, to help develop interest in the sport in China.

The Beijing center would join the centers in Wuxi, Changzhou, and Nanjing in the quest to develop baseball talent in the country.

Harold had gladly accepted the figurehead position, and had worked in the preseason to help the center get off the ground.

Although he had never said it, Harold suspected that his Chinese teammate, Jing Heng, did not like the attention being cast on the American as the new face of Chinese Baseball.

Successful American ballplayers in China were the exception rather than the rule, and one person, Jing Heng, wanted to keep it that way.

Despite being the world's largest manufacturer of metal baseball bats, the main purposes for a baseball bat in China were twofold.

One, for protection, and two, for mob use in a contract killing or to instill fear in merchants who refused to pay protection money.

Basketball and soccer were much more popular than baseball in China.

The Beijing Ducks, one of the ten teams in the Northern Division, were always perennial competitors for the Chinese Basketball Association Championship.

They played at Shougang Stadium, in front of screaming, rabid, sold-out crowds, one of whom was Harold's wife, Akemi.

Sometimes Harold thought it would be better if he were a basketball player rather than a baseball player.

The Beijing Guoan professional team was also a rousing success, placing near the top of the Chinese Super League professional soccer standings.

They were widely followed, averaging almost forty-one thousand paid fans per match in their home location, Workers Stadium.

In the years in which they were contending for the title, they would fill the sixty-six thousand seats to capacity.

The months leading up to the start of the season had been enjoyable ones for Harold and Akemi.

Harold had acclimated himself to his new surroundings in Beijing, and had gotten off to a good start in his career with the Tigers.

Akemi's job at the rape crisis center was enjoyable, fulfilling, and had given her a chance to utilize the skills she had learned through her newly acquired Masters' degree.

The couple enjoyed their new apartment, which was provided as part of Harold's first contract with the Tigers, as it was located close enough to the ballpark that, despite Akemi's concerns, Harold could relax and walk to work.

It was also close to Akemi's office, which made for an easy drive, out of rush hour traffic, each morning.

Akemi's parents had grown to like Harold more and more each day, as they watched how nicely he treated her.

His love for her was obvious, which pleased the traditional Chinese parents very much.

They dared not mention it, as it was the couple's business, but the grandparents looked forward to the day when footsteps of little grandchildren would be heard as they played in their home.

That thought had not crossed Harold and Akemi's mind yet, but someday, they would accomplish that task.

In three days, the journey to the goal of returning to major league baseball would continue.

Chapter 15

"How was your day?"

April 5

IT HAD BEEN a beautiful day to open the baseball season, with the Beijing Tigers playing the Guangdong Leopards in the warm Spring sunshine.

The publicity about Harold's debut had been over the top, which caused many curious fans to come to the ballpark to see what skills the American had brought with him.

Every seat was filled with screaming fans, including the Vice-President of the country, who was asked to throw out the first ball in the opening ceremony.

Harold's first time at bat was less than spectacular, as he was called out on a high curveball.

As he headed to the bench, Harold told himself "It is the same here as in Japan. I had better be swinging if I have two strikes."

The second time up was another disappointment, as he struck out again, this time on a sinking fastball on the outside corner.

He had endured that before, and knew that each at bat would be a new start.

Akemi and her parents sat quietly in their box seats, waiting for Harold to do something positive his third time at bat.

The Leopards were leading four to two in the bottom of the fifth, when Harold came up with two runners on base.

A two-seam fastball headed to the plate, then to the sweet spot-on Harold's bat, then toward right center field, then into the stands.

As Harold touched home plate, he felt relaxed, and the pressure of being tapped as the leader of the team by the newspapers disappeared.

Scott Binder had reached his limit on terms of pitching effectiveness, and was taken out after the fifth inning.

He would be the winning pitcher if the Tigers could play out the string as it stood.

Exhausted, he sat down on the bench to watch Harold and his teammates hopefully protect the lead for his victory.

In the eighth inning Jing Heng added a solo home run to extend the score to six to four.

The Tigers closer retired the Leopards in the ninth inning, to preserve the win for the Tigers and Scott Binder.

After the game, Akemi and her parents met Harold and made plans to visit in a few days at the Vice-Presidential residence.

He had smiled and kissed Akemi, and then had talked with her parents about the details of their upcoming visit.

Before leaving, the Vice-President, Harold's father-in-law, said "Harold, we were afraid the results would be the same as when I saw play you in New York."

Harold laughed and said, "That jinx is defeated now so it hopefully won't happen again.

But there are no guarantees it will never revisit us, as strikeouts are part of the game. Good pitchers have a way of causing that to happen."

Harold had enjoyed his comeback attempts over the last two years, but the game against the opening day game against the Leopards was a special thrill, as he had driven in the winning run-in front of a loyal, but demanding, group of fans.

Also, the game gave him special pleasure, as he was the starting catcher for the first time in over three years.

He was thrilled to be behind the plate, and look out at the field with a catcher's perspective, as the only player who faces the rest of the field, while all others look toward home plate.

His special thoughts about catching related to his father, and all that he had taught him from the time was a little league player about playing the position.

Harold loved catching. He had been ready when the Leopards tried to test his arm, and had attempted to steal second base two times during the game.

He had thrown both runners out by ten feet. He had always known that when his throws were waist high to the second baseman or shortstop who was covering the base, that he was at his best.

His smile beneath his mask was stretched from ear to ear, as he knew he was back, and would be on his way to the major leagues sooner, rather than later. The last time he had felt this alive on a baseball field was many years ago.

The couple was given a ride back to their apartment by her parents, after which they said their goodbyes, then walked up one flight of stairs above the lobby to the first floor, and to their apartment, number one hundred.

As had been the case in Japan, bodyguard Yong Wei's apartment was next to the couple's, in order to provide him quick access to protect Akemi if any danger should arise.

Once inside the door, Harold wheeled Akemi around, and kissed her passionately, then told her "Honey, we need to celebrate."

With that comment, he then led Akemi into the bedroom where they passionately passed the next hour locked in each other's arms.

Relaxed, the couple talked about how happy they were, and how much they were enjoying being in Beijing.

At one point, Harold wanted to ask Akemi a question. "I want to know about your work Akemi. How was your day?"

"Harold, I love what I am doing. Today was another day of research. I have found out something very interesting."

"What was it?"

"As I mentioned the other day, I am researching rape in China."

"Yes, I remember."

"Rape is rarely reported in China. Over twenty two percent of males, living in urban and rural areas of the country have admitted they forced females to have unwanted sex with them.

Most men do not admit that they have committed rape."

"I can understand why they don't."

"Fifty-five, percent of the same men admitted they had raped more than one time."

"I would think that is a very high number."

"Yes, it is. And, nine percent of those males have admitted to raping more than four women."

"That is terrible."

"Our crisis centers hear about a very low percentage of the rapes which are committed."

"Why is that?"

"If a rape has been committed by a man who is an official of the government, or by a man of high social standing, women rarely report the that the act took place."

"Why is that the case?"

"The conviction rate in general is low, and for men in a powerful position, the reality of being held accountable is extremely low."

"Do the women victims have access to the support system your center offers?"

"We have hot lines and our staff but few women take advantage of those services."

"How does the situation compare to the United States?"

"The reported rape rate is twelve times higher in America than here in China."

"That's hard to believe."

"Yes, it is. But the statistics from America's Justice Department point out that only three percent of the rapists are ever punished."

"That's terrible."

"Yes, it is. Harold, I have found out something very interesting, and also perplexing."

"What is it?"

"I have found a connection between what may be a man who is suffers from sexual sadism disorder in specific months of the year, and is a serial rapist the other months of the year."

"Please explain that to me."

"Sexual sadism involves algolagnia, which is the gaining sexual pleasure from forcing suffering, bondage, or humiliation on a woman."

"How is that done?"

"It is connected to the aggressor's fantasies, urges, and behaviors."

"How do they act out?"

"Usually, they employ techniques such spanking, whipping, cutting, tying up the victim, or strangulating them."

"Oh, my, that is so sick."

"Yes, it's terrible."

"How many of these sick people are involved in this type of action?"

"They have to have a prolonged and reoccurring practice of enjoying this practice, so the actual percentage is hard to measure."

"Do they end up murdering their victims?"

"That can happen if the aggressor escalates to a higher need of violence in order to get their pleasure and tension release."

"Oh, my."

"These types of actions are usually punished by placing the aggressor in a mental hospital rather in prison."

"How does a rapist differ from a person who has these problems?"

"A rapist commits a sexual assault, with an instance of unwanted intercourse or penetration for the victim."

"That is terrible also."

"Yes. Usually, physical force is involved, but it can also be a result of an abuse of authority where women who are subordinates of a man in a higher work level are taken advantage of, against their will."

"What are the long-term damages to these women?"

"They can suffer physical injury, psychological damage, or TSD."

"Do you mean posttraumatic stress disorder, similar to what our military heroes can suffer?"

"Yes."

"I understand the difference between the two types of concepts. I also see where rape is a criminal act, and sexual sadism is a mental problem, with two different punishments, or cures."

"Good. My research has found what I believe is a man who is a sexual sadist certain months of the year, and then becomes a rapist in the other months."

"He is really messed up."

"Yes. It rarely happens."

"It looks like either, or both, of the man's problems could lead to him becoming a killer."

"Yes, a serial killer."

"What are the details of what you found in the research?"

"I have found many victims. Their statements have shown that the man is a sexual sadist from November through March. And, it also shows that the man becomes a serial rapist from April through October."

"He sounds pretty dangerous, a powder keg ready to explode."

"Yes, that is the fear I have."

"Did you find anything else in the victim's statements?"

"Yes."

"How alarming was it?"

"Terribly alarming, with a potential for unlimited serial murders until he is caught."

"How will you try to use your data to help catch him, before he flips out and becomes a killer?"

"I have reread all of the victims' statements and I think I know what profession he works in, and the occupations in which his preferred victims are employed."

"That would be very helpful to the police."

"Yes."

"What did you determine from the data?"

"He is a human relations employee, probably in large corporation, with access to many possible victims who also work in human resource jobs."

"On what do you base that theory?"

"Several factors helped me determine that all of the victims work in that field."

"Perhaps he worked with them, or had access to a professional organization where the victims were members."

"Yes, that is what I thought also. Harold."

"What else did you find?"

"In all of the rape cases which took place from April through October, the victim was told that he would not hurt her if she was cooperative."

"What else did you find?"

"And, he said the same phrase in each case. As he was raping them, he said "HR Baby!""

"HR for Human Resources."

"Yes, the Human Resources Department."

"Were the times of the rapes usually the same?"

"Yes. They took place after midnight."

"Did any of the victims work with each other?"

"Yes. Usually, the guy would rape several girls from the same company, all of whom worked in Human Resources.

"What happened then?"

"He then would go to another company, rape several girls from the HR department in that company, and go on to the next company."

"In what cities?"

"From all over, but mainly in the Beijing, Tianjin, Guangdong, Jiangsu, Shanghai, Henan, and Shandong areas."

"There must be hundreds of victims?"

"Yes."

"How many years has this gone on?"

"Six years, as far as I can tell from our records."

"What are you going to do now?"

"I have given my basic information to the police, and told them I going to try to find out more information about the rapist."

"Honey, you are on to something in this mystery. Keep working on it."

"Thank you for listening to my thoughts, Harold."

"You're welcome. You can talk to me about that situation, or anything else you want, at any time."

"That is sweet, Harold."

"There is a charge for it though."

"What is that?'

"This."

After that comment, Harold kissed Akemi. One kiss led to another, and soon the couple was again making love, until they passed out in each other's arms.

Chapter 16

"By plane"

April 6

SHIN KOHAHU, THE long-time head of the Sumiyoski Kai branch of the Yakuza crime family, the main rival for the Yamaguchi Gumi family's control of the Yakuza organization, had feuded with now dead Daisuke Hayato for many years.

He had ordered the hit on Daisuke and his wife, as he had determined the old man was weak, the daughter and heir apparent to the throne had been murdered, and the surviving son, Masaru, had not proven he could ascend to the head of the family.

Despite being a ruthless murder and leader of a powerful crime family, Shin was a gentle man when he was out of the office.

His main love was the tending of his bonsai trees, which provided time for contemplation, his ingenuity in design, and recognition of his love and tending for the small trees which were grown in containers.

Many different styles of tree trunks were available, including the formal upright, the chokkan, informal upright, the moyogi, slant-style, the shankan, cascade-style, the kengai, and Shin's favorite choice, the sem-cascade-style, the han kengai.

Of the many styles of tree trunk styles available, Shin preferred the forest, the yose ue option, which entailed planting more than one species of tree in the tray-like pot.

He also liked small sized trees in the Komono one-handed class, which was six to ten inches tall.

Shin had been engrossed in the intricate tending of his miniature trees when he noticed a movement to his right, then one to his left. Turning around, he was startled to see four men, all holding baseball bats, facing him, not more than ten feet away.

His .38 caliber pistol, used for protection was on the end table in the family room, far away from his position in the kitchen.

He did not bother to ask why his unwanted visitors were present, and was aware that he was in an unescapable situation.

Shin would fight, and try to take some of his attackers with him. He did his best, landing several kicks and karate chops to the abdomens and bodies of the four men, but he was soon brought to a crouched position by a blow to his right knee.

Three men landed blows to his shoulders, arms, stomach, and shoulders, while a fourth attacker, a tall, muscular man, with a dark black mustache and hair, watched, as if critiquing his three subjects' technique.

When Shin had been rendered harmless, the fourth man walked towards him, bent down, looked him in the eyes, and asked if he was ready to join his ancestors.

A powerful blow landed on the victim's head, crushing his skull, and killing him instantly.

As blood flowed from Shin's head onto the floor, the fourth man lifted his baseball bat and repeated the gruesome process three more times.

The four blows had turned Shin's head into a mass of material that looked like pumpkin pie mix. The killing had been slow and torturous at first, and then swift and instantaneous at the end.

A call was made to Masaru Hayato, informing him that revenge had been extracted from the head of the Sumiyoski Kai family for the assassination of his father and mother.

Instructions were given to the fourth attacker to return with his team to Tokyo, and then report to the family business office for further instructions concerning his next assignment.

Upon arriving at the business office, the fourth man announced to the front lobby receptionist that he was [resent and ready to see Masaru Hayato when he was available.

After taking a seat in the lobby, he waited patiently for ten minutes, meditating until he was called into Masaru's office.

"Isamu Goro, please come in."

"Hello, sir."

"Welcome back."

"Thank you."

"I am very proud of you and your team's results in your recent assignment."

"It was my honor, sir."

"I am very satisfied with the outcome, and the manner in which it was carried out."

"We did as you wanted, with a slow, painful attack, and a swift, instant death at the end of the attack."

"Did he suffer?"

"Yes."

"How much?"
"It was a very painful experience for him."
"Did he try to fight back?"
"Yes."
"Very good. He felt as my parents did then, when he ordered that type of death for them."
"Yes, he was humbled."
"Was here fear in his eyes at any point?"
"Yes, especially at the end, when I lowered my bat for the killing blow."
"Excellent! You did what was ordered."
"Yes. It was an enjoyable experience for me also."
"That is one quality I love about you Isamu. You thoroughly enjoy your work."
"Thank you. It is what I enjoy most in life."
"Are you ready for your next assignment?"
"Yes."
"As we have talked, you will be heading to China, to eradicate Mr. Harold Gatewood."
"In what manner?"
"In any manner you choose."
"Very good."
"You can make it slow and painful, or quick. It is totally up to your discretion."
"The main thing is that it must be done successfully."
"I understand."
"Gatewood has been a root cause of my parents, and sister's deaths."
"I know."
"Revenge is the key word. We must make him pay for his actions."
"He will."
"He is playing baseball in China."
"Yes, I heard that."
"He is living in Beijing."
"Yes."
"He has followed his usual pattern, living near the ballpark. He has also kept his habit of walking to the ballpark each day he is in Beijing."
"Old habits die hard, sir."
"We hope to count on that when we take him out."
"I understand."

"He lives a simple, quiet life. He spends his time at the ballpark, or with his wife, who is his best friend. He is a family man, but he only has a wife, as they have no kids."

"What about our contacts in Beijing?"

"We have a very small network of supporters in China."

"What kind of assistance will they provide me?"

"They will provide you basic lodging and a car."

"Are they versed in military type tactics?"

"No, they are just loyalists."

"Will the planning and details be my responsibility?"

"Yes."

"Can more assistance be found?"

"Yes. I have paid our usual support person to assist you in any mission related area you need."

"What kind of help can he provide me?"

"He has access to information which can be invaluable."

"What about weaponry?'

"He can help you with that type of need."

"What if I am captured or arrested?"

"He can help you if you suffer those fates."

"What is my cover?"

"You will be traveling as a salesman for our legitimate business, in the exercise equipment industry."

"Will I be operating solo, or will I be joined by another member of the enforcement arm of our family?"

"You will be working as a solo agent."

"How long do you anticipate the mission lasting?"

"There is no time limit for the mission. There is only one requirement."

"And that is what?"

"That Gatewood be killed."

"I will make sure that happens. How will I communicate with you?"

"Please use your usual means of contact. Do not trust your loyalists too much, as I think that they may be afraid of the Chinese military and the government."

"I understand."

"Are there any more questions?"

"Not on the purpose of the mission."

"Good. The only thing that matters is killing Gatewood. You have complete freedom to accomplish that task."

"How will I be entering China?"

"By plane."

"Thank you, sir."

After the completion of the meeting, Isamu Goro returned home, and readied himself for the mission.

He was restless, having spent two weeks of inactivity after his baseball bat bludgeoning of the head of the Sumiyoski Kai family crime boss, and wanted to get back on the job.

The mentally-touched, psychopath. had missed the act of killing, He was ready to add Harold Gatewood's name to his list of victims.

Chapter 17

"I am Ready"

April 6

HE HEADED UP the stairs of the old, style, Spanish home in the old section of Madrid, on his way to what he hoped would turn out to be his destiny.
Since he had been a little boy, he had dreamed of this opportunity.

His dreams had magnified with the success of his two cousins from Vitoria, as they had become local heroes to the people in the area of the country where he lived.

His pace had quickened as he sprang up the flight of stairs, taking two steps with each bound of his legs.

Soon, his was on the second floor of the nondescript office of the AIO National Headquarters.

The office had no sign on the door identifying the nature of its business, nor any listing of the officers of in its organization.

The organization operated in secret, and out of the way of the government.

When he had knocked on the door, an eye had viewed his presence through the peep hole, where upon the door had been opened, and he was granted entry.

The outer room of the building was darkly lit, and had a bland appearance, with walls barren of pictures and any other items which would give a visitor a hint of what went on inside.

He had been led through a narrow hallway to a large room in the back of office, where he had then followed his escort to a large, long, rectangular table.

Before sitting down, he looked at the eight men sitting around the table, aware that while he did not know their names, he did know who they were, as they were the eight men who had raised their hands in approval of his carrying out the mission, Operation Tiger Slayer.

He then gazed at the walls of the room, noticing several framed pictures of former Basque patriots and freedom fighters who had faithfully served the cause, some with the forfeiture of their lives.

His eyes had stopped at two pictures in particular, those of Bakar and Bittor Kemen, of Vitoria.

These men had been his heroes, and while they were gone, they would forever be the motivation for his currently assigned mission. In addition, they had been his cousins.

He was urged to take a seat in the open chair in front of him by a wave of the hand of the man sitting at the head of the table, below the beautiful Ikurrina, in the Basque language, flag.

It sported a bright red background, a large green X from each corner through the middle of the flag, and a while cross superimposed on the top of the symbols.

It was an inspiring sight, one which highlighted the Basque people's struggle for freedom, and one which made his visit seem more important.

Ekain Koldo, the National Commander for the AIO terrorist organization, the Deputy National Commander, and the ten members representing the five regions of the organization had waited to take their seats until he had done so.

The National Commander opened the meeting with the comments to the assembled contingent.

"Welcome Basque freedom fighters to our meeting."

Twelve pairs of hands pounded on the table in approval of Koldo's comments.

"Comrades, our organization has been damaged by a scourge of a man who has caused our people and this organization much embarrassment and despair. Our membership demands revenge."

"We agree."

"Our revenge is down because of this man. He has humiliated us through his actions. He has shamed us for not stopping his resistance to our attempts to kill him."

"Sadly so, sir."

"Comrades, we voted for the approval of our agent, Eneko Itzal, to right these wrongs against the Basque people. Comrades, he is here this evening. Welcome."

"Thank you, sir, for inviting me."

"You are welcome, Eneko. But, the invitation comes with needed assurances that you are the man who can accomplish the mission with which we have entrusted to you.

"I understand, sir."

"Your success is imperative to our goals."

"I understand that also, sir."

"Do you know the history of the damage this enemy of the Basque people, Harold Gatewood, has heaped upon them since he entered their sphere of life?"

"Yes, sir. I lived through, and studied about, the events our enemy has caused."

"We know that he killed your cousins, Bakar and Bittor Kemen. You have done your homework well. And, you have reasons beside your personal desire for revenge, to accomplish this reason."

"Yes. I was in the crowd in Plaza Constitutional, when he opened the Festival of San Fermin from the terrace of the Ayuntamiento. I could have killed him there myself, but I was not assigned the mission."

"You were not ready then."

"You can rest assured I am now."

"We agree."

"What are my instructions?"

"You will be our operative for Operation Tiger Slayer. We ask you to take revenge for our three operatives who failed to eliminate him, and for all of our operatives who have lost their lives, or have been imprisoned."

"I will do so, with pleasure."

"You are to travel to China, arriving in Beijing, as a businessman who is an importer of Chinese casual wear clothing,

You have become well versed in the details of the line of sweaters, t-shirts, sweatshirts, sweatpants, and jackets that you will be supposedly be representing as part of your cover, in case you are asked to present your qualifications as an importer, right?"

"Yes, I have mastered that information."

"You are, in theory, looking for a manufacturer to produce your goods in China. This cover will allow you to travel in the country without alerting anyone of your mission."

"Yes Sir."

"You have also mastered the concepts of cost, quality, and shipping arrangements necessary for your clothing line, which will allow you to be in coastal shipping centers in China."

"I understand."

"Our organization is almost nonexistent in China, so we have arranged to use a contact there who will assist you with housing, transportation, and any weaponry you may require."

"Yes, sir."

"Here is his cell phone number."

"Thank you."

"Do not ever call him on any other number, as he must remain unknown, and not connected to our mission."

"I understand."

"Your mission is to follow the target, and take him out in any manner you deem necessary. Ideally, it should be done in a manner where no attention is drawn to you, or the AIO after it is completed, and you are safely out of the country."

"I understand."

"The target is a clean liver. He does not drink, smoke, or go to bars. He is married, and his wife is his best friend, the one whom he spends his time with as often as he can."

"I understand."

"He is athletic, knows some self-defense methods, and can defend himself. To our knowledge, he does not carry a firearm, but that fact may have changed recently."

"I understand."

"You have killed before, with three civilian kills."

"Three reported kills, sir. I was adept in four others so no connection was made to my efforts."

"You do not have any reservations then about killing whomever you deem necessary?"

"No sir, I rather enjoy it."

"We have a couple concerns."

"What are they?"

"We know that you like the ladies."

"Yes, sir, I certainly do."

"What were the details of your killing of the South Korean female agent?"

"It was an accident."

"Keep your nose clean. We don't want any outside recreational activities with females to place your mission in peril."

"I will not allow that to happen, sir."

"Also, we understand your hatred for the target, based on his killing of your two cousins. Do not let that hatred prevent you from using good judgement in your mission."

"I will not make that mistake."

"We also want you to keep a very low profile."

"I will."

"When your mission is completed, our contact will help assist your extraction from China."

"How will that happen?"

"You will take a boat to Japan, where you will go to Tokyo for a flight to Paris. From there, you will be driven to the Vitoria area, then back here for a briefing, and an update with us at this location."

"I understand."

"Eneko, do you have a blood lust to kill this target?"

"Yes, sir, I do. I want revenge for my family, and for the Basque people. I want to prove that I am fit for further missions."

"Very good. You have been unanimously approved for this crucial mission. We are counting on you."

"I will not disappoint you."

"Kill Gatewood, or you will not leave China alive."

"I will kill him, sir. I am ready."

Chapter 18

Three Month Review

April 6

HE HAD BEEN running late all morning, and he had gotten stuck in traffic, forcing him to phone the office to inform them of his situation.

Of all days to be late the first time for his job, he had picked the wrong day, as today was his first three-month, performance, review.

He scurried down the hall toward the office of his mentor, Rick Owens, who had also been promoted to his position as Director of the CIO on the same day as the late arriving employee had taken over as Deputy Director.

He had come from a family of diplomats, as his grandfather had served as the Ambassador to Argentina, and his Father had served in a similar position in Chile and Paraguay.

He had been a track star in high school in Arlington, Virginia, and then at the University of Virginia in Charlottesville.

He had been a hurdler, in both the low and high hurdle events, and had transferred the skill of hurdling obstacles to his career in the CIO.

After training at Quantico Marine Base in Virginia, and a stint as a team leader on a LRRP team, he conducted long-range reconnaissance missions far inside enemy lines.

He was heavily, decorated, for his squad's number one, kill rate in the history of the marine corps, and for bravery beyond the call of duty.

His CIO career started after the end of his Marine Corps enlistment, when he served as a supervisor of analysts in the drug and narcotics area, helping develop a streamlined information system which helped to identify drug lords worldwide.

A promotion to an internal position at the main CIO headquarters in Fairfax, Virginia, followed, after which he was chosen to be the Ambassador to Guatemala, before returning to headquarters to serve in his current position.

His career had been varied, which had allowed him to understand how the various departments in the agency worked; It had also been wildly successful.

He knocked on the door, and entered Rick Owens office.

"Hello, sir. I was stuck in traffic, and couldn't get here until now."

"We got your message. I had the same problem, and just got here five minutes ago. Let me get organized for our meeting."

"Fine, sir."

"Are you a baseball fan, Terry?"

"Yes."

"So, am I. Do you ever go to the Nationals games?"

"Yes. About five or six times a year."

"Terry, today we will go over the standard questions on the three-month review form."

"Okay."

"Have you acquainted yourself with the people who run each American embassy?"

"Yes."

"Are you familiar with the reporting procedures?"

"Yes."

"Is there any aspect of your job responsibilities which you are unsure of, and need assistance or training?"

"No."

"What is covered in an incident report?"

"Any developments in countries which would cause the CIO to be aware of now, or in the future, events which might negatively impact the United States, should be included in the report.

Our mission here is to do what?

"To protect the citizens of the United States against threats, foreign and domestic."

"We specialize in what?"

"Gathering overseas intelligence and information, and limited domestic information is our charge, sir."

"Do we have a law enforcement function?"

"No."

"What do we do with the information we gather?"

"We process and analyze the data to determine if there is a potential national security risk in any location in the world.

We watch for bad things which may happen. We try to stay ahead of the possibility of those things happening."

"What is HUMIT?"

"It stands for Human Intelligence information gathering, which is our best way of performing our mission."

"What can we do in the area of covert action on behalf of the president of the country?"

"Sir, we have to be careful, as there are things we can and can't due legally."

"Correct. By law, we can oversee these covert activities. Unless?"

"Unless the president chooses another agency, he thinks can do the job better than we can."

"Can we exert political influence through our tactical divisions?"

"Yes."

"Please name one of our tactical divisions."

"The Special Activities Division."

"Correct. What has happened to the CIO since the terrorist attack on September 11, 2001?

"The CIA Director transferred some of his powers in the intelligence area to the Director of National Intelligence."

"And, what else?"

"The agency has shown positive growth and results."

"What about our budget?"

"It has grown, with positive improvement in the per dollar invested metric, and it is the largest budget of all of the intelligence community agencies."

"Very good Terry. You know the needed basics at this point in time."

"Thank you."

"Can we conduct covert paramilitary operations?"

"Yes."

"What about nonconsensual human experiments?"

"Yes Sir, we can do those."

"Can we abduct and extra judiciously transfer a person from one county to another?"

"Yes."

"What is that practice called?"

"Extraordinary rendition"

"Can we use enhanced interrogation techniques?"

"Yes."

"Please name on such technique."

"Water boarding."

"It is a touchy subject because of what reason, Terry?"

"It has been called a terror technique."

"Can we use targeted killings?"

"Yes."

"One recent method of doing so is called what?"

"Death by use of drones."

"Can we provide military personnel to train and fund other countries' militants, to carry out a mission?"

"Yes."

"Very good. You know the handbook related to the CIO's main operational procedures."

"Thank you."

" What else do you have for me this morning, Terry?"

"Special Agent Fermin Zuzen of the Agence de Renseignement forwarded a message this morning."

"What about?"

"He has news about Harold Gatewood."

"Oh, no, not Gatewood again. What is it now?"

"There are rumblings that the AIO has been training an operative for another mission that involves Gatewood."

"Do they know where he is?"

"Yes."

"He is playing baseball in Beijing, China, correct?"

"Yes,"

"No doubt they will send an operative to terminate him."

"They have tried many times before so I would agree with your comment, sir."

"We will have to take action on that matter."

"Sir, Agent Zuzen also said that the Yakuza, in Japan, also is now aware of Gatewood's presence in China and may also send someone to even the score with him"

"How can we help him, Terry?"

"He has already become the face of baseball in China. Taking into account his history with the AIO, and the Yakuza, his death could create problems for us, and possibly for Japan and China."

"In the past, we have sent an agent to oversee the situation, and try to protect Gatewood, and our country's interests."

"I think we should do that again."

"There is one other factor in the scenario."

"What is it?"

"Gatewood is now married to the daughter of the Vice-President of China, Guo Gang."

"He has a knack for embroiling himself in the most unfortunate circumstances. He is potentially in the middle of a deteriorating diplomatic relationship between China and Japan."

"Yes, sir. China has showed increased military force in the East and South, China Seas."

"Okay. We will send one of our top operatives, Jack Taylor, to China to protect Harold Gatewood, and to prevent his death from becoming a nasty development between the two countries."

"I think that is a wise action."

"Make it happen, immediately, Terry."

"I will."

"Contact our Ambassador in the American Embassy, Roger Caldwell, about our plans for Jack Taylor and Harold Gatewood."

"I will."

"Terry, you are doing a fine job of grasping your role here at the CIO."

"Thank you. sir."

"Keep me posted on the Gatewood situation."

"I will."

Chapter 19

"Like a clock?"

April 6

AS A LITTLE boy, he had worked in the rice fields with his father and mother.

It was grueling work, especially for a young boy, but it hardened him with a steel determination to make something of himself, and escape the poverty into which he had been born.

He used to hit bugs off of the rice plants with a stick, which helped him develop excellent hand and eye coordination.

As he became older, he would imagine he was anywhere else but where he lived, so strong was his desire to start a different life, one which would allow him to reach his now unknown destiny.

He had grown into a hulk of a young man, tall, strong, and muscular. His build and skills would lead him to a career which was unrelated to anything he might have imagined, one which would pay him handsomely, and make him a national hero.

The strong youth had the world by the tail, except for one fatal flaw, one which would endanger his success and freedom.

As he stood silently, watching the light in the window above him, his muscles tensed with anticipation of what pleasure lay ahead of him.

He enjoyed the act of preparing his victim, and in the actual performance of the sex act.

The powerful man had spent time planning his entrance, and would soon walk up the stairs after entering the back door, which he had left unlocked earlier in the evening.

He had watched the door to make sure no one had entered it from the street, or had shut and locked it from the basement inside.

A uniform of black clothing, augmented with a black face mask, and latex gloves, which would prevent the leaving of his fingerprints, would eliminate the possibility of him from being seen, or recognized.

He would carry a small bag, which was stocked with his needed tools, which included lock picking items, sanitary wipes, duct tape, a handkerchief to stuff in the victim's mouth, a cocktail mix of zolpidem and flunitrazepam, a syringe to administer the drugs, and condoms.

Zolpidem was excellent for incapacitating the victim, which would allow him to ample time to enjoy the sexual act which would follow.

A normal, prescribed, dosage of five milligrams for a woman would create a lasting sleep for two or three hours, and would take effect within fifteen minutes after injection.

His cocktail mix was much stronger, and would knock the victim out much quicker than the regular dosage.

The flunitrazepam, more commonly called rhino, would augment the effects of the zolpidem, and quickly help sedate the victim.

Hallucinations, amnesia, and incapacitation were the immediate effects on the victim.

After-effects of both drugs included headache, nausea, vomiting, confusion, sluggishness, poor physical and mental coordination, and a hangover feeling.

Presence of the drugs could be detected by a blood test within twenty-eight hours of initial injection.

Both drugs were available and easily obtainable from manufacturers in the England.

The presence of alcohol, combined with the drugs, created a magnified effect, and shortened the time before the victim became incapacitated.

He had studied the victim's habits, and knew that she would have visited happy hour with her fellow Human Resources department co-workers on the night of his planned attack.

Once inside the building he had walked up the stairs to her apartment door, used his locking picking tools, a pick gun, which enhanced quick and easy lock picking, and a torsin wrench, which was used to turn the plug of the lock once the pins were held in place, to gain entry into the living room.

He then used a credit card to lift the chain lock on the inside of the door.

Once he was able to grab the chain with his fingers, he had then slid it out of its hole, and down the short groove, catching it as it fell downward into his other hand.

He was in. He then silently walked to the victim, lying in a drunken condition, on the bed.

The attacker then placed his hand over her mouth to prevent her from screaming, then told her to remain quiet, and that he would not hurt her unless she resisted his actions, or tried to call for help.

He then took the syringe, loaded with his cocktail mix of incapacitating drugs, from his bag, and injected the potion into the victim's right arm.

While she soon passed into a state of semi-consciousness, almost unable to move, he had seen the looks of fear, panic, and confusion in her eyes.

Once she was sedated, he had taken the alcohol laced wipes from his bag, and cleaned every inch of her prone body.

When finished, he then proceeded to fondle and caress the beautiful woman before him.

He had run his hands along her body from head to toe, making a stop in her lower private area.

He then put on a condom, and proceeded to rape the victim. When satisfied, he then cleaned the victim, inside and out, with more of the wipes.

Before leaving, he took a final glance at the woman on the bed in front of him.

He was proud of himself, as he had chosen a very nice subject with which he could satisfy his control and sexual needs.

She was tall, at five-feet-seven, inches, had short black hair, dark eyes, soft skin, a smooth complexion, perfect white teeth, long legs which he had wrapped around himself during the sex act, large breasts which had kissed, one at a time, and beautiful hands, with long fingers.

After a smile had graced his face, he had gathered the items of his rape kit, and slowly exited the apartment, closing the door behind him as he left.

Once down the back stairs, and outside of the apartment building, he had walked into the darkness and headed home, his mission accomplished.

He would sleep late into the morning the following day, arise, eat a huge brunch, and then walk to his place of employment, where he would be cheered by thousands to play a little boy's game.

The victim also slept late into the following morning, but arose to a state of confusion and dizziness.

After feeling nauseous, vomiting, and suffering from a massive headache, the victim, Shu Yun, whose name meant Gentle Cloud, did not feel like she represented the meaning of either one of her names.

She was not feeling gentle, and even in her confused condition, knew that she wanted to seek revenge on the large, heavy man who had almost crushed her when he had laid on her body during the rape.

The young lady was also not feeling like a cloud, one which soared above the earth in a relaxed, easy-going manner, as she was feeling terrible, and wanted medical help to conquer the storms which were brewing inside her body.

She had staggered from her bed, and then called for an ambulance to take her to the nearby hospital. She was in bad shape, and she knew it.

Akemi Gatewood, had been working at her desk when she received the call requesting that she come to the hospital to interview a rape victim.

As she had done many times before, she told her assistant that she was needed at the hospital, and would be back later.

After being directed to the room where Shu Yun was recuperating, Akemi had entered, introduced herself, and asked if she could talk to the victim, who agreed.

"Shu Yun, I am Akemi Gatewood. I am with the Rape Crisis Center. May I speak with you?"

"Yes."

"Thank you. How are you feeling?"

"I am very weak and disoriented."

"I know what you are going through. I am here to help you."

"Thank you."

"What do you remember about last night?"

"I went out to celebrate my co-worker's birthday with members of my Human Resources Department."

"Did you have any alcohol last night?"

"Yes."

"What happened then, Shu?"

"I went home, and laid down on the bed, as I had too much to drink at the restaurant."

"And then what happened?"

"I passed out."

"For how long?"

"Three or four hours."

"Then what happened?"

"I felt someone putting their hand on my mouth."

"Did you struggle?"

"No, because the man told me he would hurt me if I screamed, or tried to get away."

"What happened after that?"

"He injected me with something. He used a syringe."

"Did you feel sick afterwards?"

"I felt sleepy, and did not know where I was, or what was happening. I was in and out of consciousness."

"What do you remember?"

"He cleaned me off with wipes. I could smell and feel the alcohol on my body."

"Do you mean wipes like those used on babies?"

"Yes, baby wipes."

"What happened after that?"

"He felt me, all over my body."

"In what way?"

"He ran his hands all over me, from my feet to my hair. He also stopped in my lower sexual area."

"Then what did he do?"

"He put on a condom and then got on top of me."

"Did he rape you?"

"Yes. Two times."

"Did he say anything to you during those times?"

"Yes, both times he said 'HR Baby.' I don't know what that means,

"HR Baby?"

"Yes, how did he know I worked in Human Resources?"

"I don't know, Shu."

"I found that comment very strange."

"I don't know what it means, Shu."

"Okay. Did you recognize the man?"

"No."

"Perhaps he looked like someone you work with, or someone you encounter in your daily life."

"Like who?"

"A person at your dry cleaners, a person who may deliver things to your work, a male hairdresser, basically, anyone you might encounter as you live each day."

"No. But there was something familiar about him, like I had seen him somewhere before."

"Maybe he was an actor, a television reporter, or someone in the public eye."

"Maybe, but I don't know."

"Shu, do you have a boyfriend?"

"No. I recently broke up with a man I had been going with for four years."

"I don't mean to pry, but what was the reason for the end of the relationship?"

"He was very jealous, and controlling."

"In what way?"

"He always wanted to know where I was, what I was doing, and if I was cheating on him."

"Were you?"

"No. I never cheated on him."

"Did he ever be violent with you?"

"Yes, one time."

"How did that happen?"

"He had followed me after work. I had run into a former co-worker who had taken another job and we had talked about how things were going for him."

"And your ex-boyfriend interrupted your conversation?"

"Yes, he caused a scene. After my ex-co-worker left, we argued, and I had told him to stop following me."

"And, he lost his temper, and hit you?"

"Yes, but it was not planned."

"That doesn't make any difference."

"I know."

"Does he still follow you?"

"No. He finally accepted our breakup."

"Was he the man who attacked you?"

"No. It was not him."

"Do you remember anything else Shu?"

"The man had four moles on his back. They were shaped like a clock."

"Shaped like a clock?"

"Yes. One was at twelve o'clock, one was at three o' clock, one was at six o'clock, and one was at nine o'clock."

"Were they large, or small moles?"

"They were small ones."

"That may be very helpful."

"Akemi, do you think he will be caught by the police?"

"I hope so."

"I hope so too."

"Was there anything else you remember?"

"Even though he was very big, and almost squashed me when he was on top of me, he seemed very gentle."

"Gentle?"

"Yes. And, he was very sure and confident in what he was doing to me, not clumsy in his actions."

"Like he had done it before?'

"Yes, like he had done it many times before."

"Shu, has anyone ever done this to you before?"

"No."

"Did the doctors tell you about their findings?"

"Yes, they told me he had used drugs to sedate me, to prevent me from fighting back."

"Yes, and those drugs will pass through your system in a few more hours, and you will regain your strength, and feel better."

"I am looking forward to that."

"Shu, is there anything else you can tell us?"

"I remember thinking that his cologne smelled familiar, and there were some catchy words I had heard about it."

"Such as a commercial?"

"Yes, maybe. Or a jingle."

"Do you remember what it smelled like?"

"No."

"Do you have someone you can stay with?'

"Yes. My sister's family."

"Maybe you should consider staying with them until you are stronger."

"Okay."

"I don't want to alarm you, but sometimes, a rapist will return to a prior victim."

"Do you think he will come back?"

"I don't know, but I would urge you to upgrade the security you have in your apartment to be on the safe side."

"I will."

"You will get through this Shu. There are many people who can help you, including me."

"Thank you."

"You can call me anytime. My cell and office phone numbers are on my card."

"Mrs. Gatewood, please help the police catch the man who did this to me."

"I will."

"I want to ask you a question Mrs. Gatewood."

"Okay."

"When I get married, do you think my husband will hold this against me?

"Of course not."

"I hope not."

"Do not worry about that. You will find, and marry, a wonderful man who will respect and love you."

"I hope so."

"He will."

"I know you are married Mrs. Gatewood. I hope you have a husband like you just mentioned."

"I do. I am very lucky. He is a wonderful man. And, you will find one also."

"Thank you, Mrs. Gatewood."

"Thank you, Shu. Get some rest now."

"I will."

As Akemi rode the elevator down to the lobby of the hospital, she thought about Shu Yun, their interview, and how much she wanted to help catch the man who had raped the young woman, and thrown her life into turmoil.

Shu Yun would need help, but she would recover. The man who committed the terrible crime would need to be apprehended before he could rape again.

Akemi vowed to do everything in her power to help bring him to justice.

Chapter 20

The Succession

April 7

AFTER HER POST-RAPE rape interview with Shu Yun the day before, Akemi could not wait to get to her office to see if the police had come up with any leads based on the information, she had forwarded them.

She was assured that they were trying, but that it was too early to expect results.

Unknown to Akemi, her office assistant had listened to her employer's phone conversation with the police, and had made notes about the rapist, thinking that the knowledge might be worth money to the right person.

Harold had gone to the ballpark for another home game with Guangdong Leopards, and was scheduled to catch once again.

It would be his third game in a row, and he was showing no aches or pain from his return to the game's hardest position.

Baseball was fun again, and Harold loved going to the ballpark, knowing he would be doing what he was born to do.

The game was a pitcher's duel, with the Tigers holding a one to nothing lead going into the bottom of the eighth inning.

The crowd had been as wound up as usual, with chants, cheers, and balloons filling the air, in the home team's seventh inning.

In the eighth inning, the crowd had become very quiet, as shocking news had been announced on the radio, and the internet.

Fans who had their small transistor radios, and their cell phones, had heard the news, and were glued to their devices to gain further information about what had happened.

The president of the country had suffered a heart attack at the Asia Pacific Economic Conference in Seoul, South Korea.

He had been rushed to the hospital, and no news had been released since that had taken place, thirty-seven minutes earlier.

The fans were on the edge of their chairs in anticipation of further news about the president's condition.

Harold's thoughts were about Akemi and her parents. The remainder of the ballgame passed quickly, and in total silence, as the country was on the edge of a catastrophe, with the transfer of political leadership on the line.

Both the bottom of the eight for the Tigers, and the top of the ninth for the Leopards, went quickly, as the six outs were recorded in order, preserving the win for the home team, one to nothing.

Harold called Akemi as soon as he was in the clubhouse, to check on her, and her parents', situations.

"Akemi, how are you?"

"I am fine Harold. Have you heard the news?"

"Some of it. What is the latest word?"

"The president is in intensive care."

"Will he survive?"

"It looks very bad from what my father has told me."

"How is your father?"

"He is shaken up, but he is fine."

"Is he at home?"

"No. he's in his office. The government is having non-stop meeting."

"How is your mother?"

"She is fine. She called me as soon as she heard the news."

"Is Yong Wei on duty near you?"

"Yes, he is in the reception room here at our office."

"Is there extra security for your parents?"

"Yes, they were dispatched to the house right away."

"And, the military is probably guarding your father."

"Yes, he is safe."

"We need to consider having more security for you if the president dies, and your father is the new leader of the country."

"We will talk about that later."

"Okay."

"When are you coming home?"

"As soon as I shower, I'll head home."

"I am almost down with my workday. I'll be home soon. Did you win today?"

"Yes, one to nothing. A close game."

"How did you do?"

"One for three."

"Did you catch?"

"Yes."

"Did you throw anyone out?"

"Yes, one runner at second base."

"Everyone will learn not to try to steal bases on you."
"So far, so good, my dear."
"Harold, I want to talk to you about something tonight?"
"What is it?"
"It is about the girl that was raped, Shu Yun."
"Sure."
"I gained some very interesting information from her."
"Okay. We'll talk tonight."
"What do you want for dinner tonight?"
"An Akemi sandwich. You, between two giant pieces of bread."
"You can have me anytime, with or without the bread."
"Fantastic."

In his office in the Zhongnanhai, the office building of the Central Government of China, and the People's Republic of China, the political and personal rival of Akemi's father, Min Jun, mulled over the probable death of the president, and how that event would impact his political career.

Min was expecting his rival, the current Vice-President, Guo Gang, to arrive any moment. Guo had requested to meet Min in light of the current president's heart attack, and to bury old grievances.

"Come in, Guo."
"Thank you, Min. Min, I appreciate you visiting with me. As you know, the president is not expected to live. It is my duty to support the office of the president. It is a bad time for all of us in government. Min."
"Yes, it is."
"It is also a bad time for the people of our country."
"I agree."
"Min, there has been bad blood between us since we were both wooing Aiko's hand for marriage."
"Yes. She chose you."
"And, we have been rivals for political offices."
"Yes, and you have beaten me every time."
"I have come to ask you to join me, in this time of crisis, to help make the probable change of leadership go smoothly."
"I understand what you need, Guo."
"Can I count on you, and your supporters, to help me?"
"Yes, for a price."
"What would that price be, Min?"
"That you appoint me Vice-President."
"I am not sure that would be best."
"It is your only hope for a smooth transition, Guo."
"I will think about it."

"Let me know, Guo."

"I will. But you realize that your choice of opening a fight at this time will not be appreciated by the Communist Party."

"Perhaps. We will have to see in whom they have the most faith.

"I wanted to come here to offer a peaceful solution to this crisis, and to best serve the people of China. Min, I am disappointed in your actions."

"It is politics, Guo. You know that."

"I will think it over, Min."

With that less-than-hopeful, outcome, Guo Gang, Akemi's father, and the soon-to-be, new president of China, headed back to his office to mend other political fences, and to address the challenges which laid ahead.

Alone in his office, Min Jun, spoke to himself, "I will appear to be supportive, but I will actually try to sabotage his every move. And, I will use any means necessary to bring about his failure. Then, I will take my rightful place as the new president of China."

Chapter 21

"I am Here"

April 7

IT WAS A beautiful spring day, with the sun shining down on the citizens of Beijing.

It was the type of day when one was happy to be alive. It was a day not to be in the office, and to enjoy time away from the doldrums of everyday life.

It was the type of day where one could be young again. It was the type of day where one did not have to go to school.

It was the type of day where one could go outside to play, imagining that they were a fireman, or a ballplayer.

Today, for Roger Caldwell, it was that type of day.

As he sat in the sun, he assessed his life, and his career. He had risen quickly in the State Department, and had earned his promotions as the Ambassador to Cuba, Japan, and now China.

He was well respected, and had a chance to meet his goal of becoming a cabinet member, or the Director of the CIO.

Roger also harbored a secret, one which he had managed to keep hidden from the government.

He had personally profited from the sale of information and access to governmental assistance to several terrorist organizations in at least three countries, Cuba, Japan, and now China.

Roger had been paid over two million dollars during his stops along the promotion trail, and looked forward to receiving more, much more, before he was ready to be put out to pasture.

He would use his talents in this area to cash in on the really big payoffs once he had reached the apex of power in Washington.

Today was not the day to think of promotions, payoffs, or power, but it was a day to sit in the sun, relax, and watch a ballgame.

Roger had made a lot of money from Harold Gatewood's attempted, career, comeback, his associations with beautiful and dangerous women, and the numerous assassination attempts on his life.

Today, Roger had succumbed to the urge to go to a Beijing Tiger baseball game. He wanted to see the man who had fueled his recent his financial windfalls.

The head of the American Embassy to China had watched the ballplayer's actions during the pregame warmup, and was struck by the professional manner in which he carried out his routine.

The ballplayer also had an infectious smile, and a pleasing personality, which sometimes interrupted his preparation.

But once the game was underway, his demeanor was all business. In fact, he played with a steely look of determination on his face, and a burning desire to hustle and win in his heart.

Some people were born to do certain things, to achieve their destiny. Harold Gatewood was born to play baseball.

Caldwell was happy that he had come to the game, to see the man whose despairs, challenges, tragedies, loves, losses, and accomplishments had become interwoven in the underground activities of the diplomat's professional career.

Roger thought to himself as the game wore on. "I am glad he is in China. His presence has led to another financial windfall for me. The AIO and the Yakuza have agreed to pay for information and assistance. Gatewood is my cash cow."

In the sixth inning Roger's cell phone rang, and brought an expected message to his ears.

"Hello, this is Eneko Itzal."

"Hello, it is nice to hear from the AIO."

"I am here."

"And, you're right on time."

"I have basic instructions already, but I do have some additional questions."

"Go ahead."

"I am at the airport. Who will be picking me up?"

"Your contact is on the way, and will be there shortly."

"How will I find him?"

"Stand outside on the curb in front of baggage claim. He will find you. He should be there in about five minutes."

"Will he be taking me to the safe house?"

"Yes."

"What about weapons?"

"They are at the safe house."

"Okay."

"Remember, I am a facilitator. If you find yourself in need of special services, such as body removal, I am the one to help."

"I understand."

"I also can help you if you get into a mess with the legal authorities, or the police.

But, if you get into a mess which requires more than my usual professional services, there will be another financial payment due from the AIO."

"I understand. I was briefed on that possibility. I have a question."

"Go ahead."

"What about the Tongs?"

"Stay away from them."

"Why? I have means of handling them. You do not."

"Okay."

"Remember that, because if you infringe on their activities while you are performing your assignment, they will kill you, or worse, you will hope that they had."

"I know how the game is played."

"Good. Do you have any other questions?"

"I do have one more question."

"What is it?"

"If I need to call again, do I use this number?"

"You must always, I repeat, always, use this number."

"I will. Thank you."

"Thank you. It is always a pleasure to do business with the AIO."

Roger Caldwell then settled back into his seat, and watched the Tigers versus Leopards game continue into the bottom of the eighth inning.

On a two ball, no strike count, Jing Heng, sometimes called "Jin Heng", or "Home Run Heng" by Harold Gatewood, hit a long, home run to left field.

As Jing Heng rounded first base, Harold noticed his teammate Scott Binder looking at him. Both knew the other's thoughts.

"Performance enhancing drugs, Scott?"

"Yes, Harold, its PED's for sure."

At the beginning of the ninth inning, with the Tigers leading one to nothing, Roger Caldwell's cell phone rang again.

"Hello, this is Isamu Goro."

"Hello. It is always nice to hear from the Yakuza."

"I am here."

"Welcome to China."

"I was instructed to call you upon my arrival."

"Yes. What can I do for you?"

"Should I wait at the airport for my ride?"

"Correct. A black sedan will pick you up in front of the terminal, baggage area C."

"Will I then go to my safe house?"

"Yes."

"Are my weapons there?"

"Yes."

"I am to contact you if I need special assistance, correct?"

"Yes."

"And, I am always to use this number?"

"Yes."

"I am all set. Thank you for your help."

'You're welcome."

In the top of the ninth inning, the Tigers had retired the first two hitters, then had run into trouble, loading the bases on two errors and a walk.

Manager Hui Jun, and Harold Gatewood, had gone to the mound to talk with the pitcher, when one more call came into Roger Caldwell's cell phone.

"Roger Caldwell?"

"Yes. Hello."

"This is Jack Taylor. I was to report in when I arrived."

"Yes, Jack. I'm happy you made it here."

"You have been briefed about my mission, correct?"

"Yes, I know why you are here."

"I will be getting settled into my safe location, unless there has been a change in plans, I am not aware of."

"There have been no changes in your plans, Jack."

"Everything I need should be at my location then?"

"Yes, everything you requested is there."

"Good. If I need anything, Roger, I will call you."

"Very good Jack. I will be here for you."

"Thanks."

"Good luck."

The Tigers had made their pitching change in an attempt to save the game. A right-handed pitcher with a mean, two-seam, fastball, proceeded to set down the last batter on three straight strikes, the last one with the hitter's bat on his shoulder.

The American Embassy head took in the sights and sounds on the field, staying in his seat until most of the other fans had left the park.

He now knew more about Harold Gatewood. He almost felt sorry for helping bring grief into the ballplayer's heart, but business was business, and

Love and Death in Beijing

he would continue to complicate the Harold's life as long as there was money to be made.

Later than evening, just before midnight, a tall, dark, muscular man dressed in black clothing, face mask, and surgical gloves, watched the five-foot-five-inch, dark, haired, dark-eyed, Human Resources employee, Qui Fen, who worked for the same company that employed Shu Yun, turn off her bedroom light, and head toward a restful sleep.

After midnight, as was his custom, the black, clad, man entered the building, then the sleeping woman's apartment, surprised her, warned her to be quiet, and then injected her with his special love cocktail, rendering her immobile.

He then proceeded in each step of his ritual, which culminated in a "HR Baby" comment once he achieved orgasm.

He then finished the after, intercourse, steps of his ritual, and left io the same path he had used to enter the building.

Once again, he had been satisfied. And, once again, he would not be apprehended by the police. He would continue to plan, and carry out, his next assaults.

Qui Fen, whose name meant Autumn Fragrance, would hope that
  the breezes of that season, would bring happier times than what the breezes of the spring had brought her on the April night of her attack.

She would stagger back to reality the next day, be admitted to the hospital for treatment related to her rape, and would reach out for someone to talk with, and to tell the details about her attacker.

That person would be Akemi Gatewood.

Chapter 22

Check the dates

April 25

THE PRESIDENT OF CHINA had died the day after suffering a massive heart attack, and the country had gone through a period of mourning caused by his death.

Akemi's father, Guo Gang, had ascended to higher office as the head of the country, and had opted for a hopeful peace within the government by supporting his arch enemy, Min Jun, as his vice-president.

The decision had been a necessary political move to stave off a crisis in the two factions of government.

In addition, Guo had been dealing with the economic problems of slowing grown and devaluation of the currency, and foreign affairs problems related to the increased friction with Japan due to the increased military type actions in the East and South China Seas.

Despite those obstacles, he was enjoying his new challenge, and was feeling great.

Akemi had become increasingly involved in the series of incidents called the HR BABY rapes. She was proving to be quite observant, and a detective in the making.

She had followed up with an additional interview with rape victim Shu Yun, who was remembering more and more details about her attacker.

Akemi had also interviewed the next woman had had been raped, Qui Fen, and had noticed many of the same details about the rapist that Shu Yun had mentioned.

She had then gone back a third time to meet with Shu Yun about the type of cologne she had smelled during the attack.

They had met at a department store near the victim's office in order to keep the attack confidential, and to check out the most popular brands of men's cologne on the market.

They had sprayed and smelled the sample bottles of each brand, hoping to identify the one the rapist wore the evening of the attack.

The spray from the first bottle had not been even close to the one which would help solve the series of rapes which had gone on for over three years.

A second, third, and fourth brand of cologne was sprayed into the air, with hopes of its scent leading to the rapist.

Nothing was unearthed in the search of the first sixteen types of men's cologne, which had caused the two women to become disappointed.

Shu Yun was ready to give up, and return to work, but Akemi had convinced her to try the three remaining brands of cologne.

The first brand, an older one which had been a big seller for years, and which had lost its market share, provided no answer.

The second brand, two years old, had flopped, and was part of an inventory which the store had taken a beating on, with only a few scant bottles being sold in a gross of one hundred forty for bottle ordered.

In fact, it had become a joke for the salespeople in the department, as each person wondered what other uses could be found for the product in order to get rid of it.

The last option, a green bottle with a gold cap, was a brand which neither Akemi or Shu Yun had ever seen before. Akemi squeezed the button which released the spray into the air, and waited for a reaction from Shu Yun.

"That's it! That's it! He was wearing that the evening he raped me."

"Are you sure?"

"Yes. I am positive. I would never forget that smell."

Both of the women were overjoyed with their discovery, and wanted the saleslady to tell them the history of the brand.

A small number of bottles, thirty in total, had been given to the store to test market its potential. The results were dismal.

Only three bottles were ever sold. Akemi asked if they could buy three bottles of the inventory, and, if possible, have a list of the three customers who had purchased the cologne, as this information might help the police solve a series of crimes.

The salesclerk said that she thought the manager of the department might have the list in her product files. After ten minutes, she returned with the list in hand.

The list contained the names, phone numbers, and addresses of the three purchasers of the cologne.

Akemi had told Shu Yun that she would contact the three buyers and see if any new information could be determined from their knowledge of the product.

The manufacturer of the product, the distributor, and the salesman who had sold the inventory to the store for market testing, were also identified, and would be contacted for information.

The manager had told the salesclerk to let the women know that the brand did not sell because it was overpriced, as an extra layer of expense was included to cover a royalty fee which would be paid to a famous spokesperson who had agreed to be the face of the product.

Unfortunately, the manager had no knowledge of identity of the celebrity who was chosen to be the product's spokesperson.

Akemi had been overjoyed, and had told Shu Yun that she was optimistic that this might be the break they needed to catch the rapist.

She had returned to the office and had made several phone calls to everyone connected with the product, without success.

The president of the company that had manufactured the product had died, and no record was found of the agreement with the spokesman.

The upper management at the distributing company has all been fired, or had quit, and had left the country for opportunities in other companies.

A flurry of phone calls had turned up nothing in terms of the two former product managers who might provide information. The salesman who worked with the department store's account had been an elderly man, who had passed away.

Akemi had been stymied in her search, but she was hopeful information on the brand's spokesperson would turn up.

She had been able to find out the name of the product, which was slated to be called Big Hitter.

It was not much, but it had been a start which she had hoped might lead to positive action in the future.

Harold and the Tigers had left on a ten-day road trip, with games with division teams, the Sichuan Dragons, Jianjin Pegasus, and their perennial rivals, the Tianjin Lions.

His roommate for road games would be his former roommate in Japan, Scott Binder.

The Tigers had gotten off to a good start on the trip, winning two of three games with each of the Dragons and Pegasus, and had headed into the final four game series, tied with the Lions.

In the first two series, in Tianjin, and Jianjin, the Tigers had gotten good run production and pitching, with Harold and "Home Run Heng", each hitting a home run on two of the three days in each of the series.

As usual, Jing Heng had pulled his disappearing act during the road trip, bolting from the bus once it returned to the team's hotel after the game, never to be seen until he boarded the bus the next day for the game.

Harold had told Scott that they needed to invent and sell a board game modeled after the "Where's Waldo" fad in the United States, which could be called "Where's Heng".

Jing Heng was always on cloud nine if he hit a homerun in a game, even if the team lost. No one knew where he went after such occasions.

Some people thought he went on a bender. Some people thought he had girlfriends in each town, and that he would snuggle up with them until it was time to board the bus for the next day's game.

The superstitious players on the team thought he became a bird and flew to the baseball Heavens to rest, and then return to play again.

Since he was awarded the star treatment, he roomed alone, so no roommate could report his comings and goings. The situation was the same in Beijing, as he was never spotted in public, refused to do interviews, and no one had ever found out where he lived.

Heng could hit, but there was a price to pay for having him around. His teammates were always at odds with each other, as they could never agree what species of poisonous snake to buy him for his birthday.

Harold respected him as a hitter, and that was it. He was a pathetic package to have around, and was a potential boiling pot of distrust and hatred which could explode at any minute.

As hard as it might have been for people to accept, Harold knew that the team would be better off without Heng's volcanic nature, his long home runs, and his runs batted in's.

But, Heng was Harold's teammate, and he could live with that, as long as it did not cause uncontrollable problems on the field.

The series with the Lions was a disaster for the Tigers, as they lost four straight, being blown out in each game.

The time to return to Beijing had arrived, and the smog-cloaked city looked very good as they landed at the airport.

Harold had been more than ready to see Akemi, make love to her, and talk to her, as he had missed her.

"Hi. Are you glad to be home?"
"Yes, I am always glad to be with you."
"You did well, except for the last series with the Lions."
"Thanks. That is over and we can start anew tomorrow."
"I have been busy."
"What progress have you made in the serial rapist case?"

"I have turned over some very good clues. I think we are getting close to identifying him."

"What clues did you find?"

"I went with Shu Yun to a department store to try to find the cologne she recognized."

"Did you find it?"

"Yes."

"What is it called?"

"Something very strange. It is called 'Big Hitter'."

"That is an unusual name. Who was it named after?"

"I don't know. Maybe it was named after a boxer."

"Does China have many boxing idols?"

"The sport has been around almost one hundred years, and we have done well in the Olympics. We finally had a world champion in minimum weight class, Xiong Zhad Zhong."

"Do you think he is the rapist?"

"No. He is a small man, and all of the reports say the rapist is a very large man."

"Is this the bottle the cologne is in?"

"Yes, smell it. It is distinctive, but it does not smell that great."

"It smells awful. No wonder no one bought it."

"You're right about that."

"The bottle looks okay."

"Yes, it is jade green with a gold top."

"What else did you find out?'

"We think that he may be under the influence of drugs, to do so many rapes over the past few years."

"Is there any other reason you think that?"

"He is adept at using needles, as he injects his victims with date rape concoctions."

"Did you find out anything about his physical traits?"

"We know that he has four moles on his back, in a clock-shaped pattern."

"What do they look like?"

"They look like numbers on a clock, at twelve, three, six, and nine o'clock."

"Really, did you tell me it was on his shoulder?"

"Yes."

"Did you find out anything about the HR Baby comment and how it relates to a Human Resources department in a company?"

"Many of the victims worked in that department for several different companies. In fact, almost all of them worked in Human resources."

"What is the connection?"

"The rapist must have connections or access to the Human Resources departments for all of the companies."

"Did you ever think that HR might represent another area, or a title, maybe even a place."

"We haven't come up with anything yet."

"Akemi, will you please come here? I want to kiss you, and make love with you."

"Hai,"

After two hours of making up for being apart for ten days, and being very worn out from their lovemaking, the couple relaxed in bed, with Akemi laying on Harold's stomach, and he having his hand on her back, rubbing her soft skin.

They talked for a few moments. Harold told Akemi he wanted to tell her something which might sound farfetched, but might be on the mark.

"Honey, I have a theory for you. I think I may know the identity of the rapist."

"Really? Tell me."

"I have seen a green bottle with the gold cap like the one you showed me."

"Where?"

"I will tell you where in a minute. Also, I have seen some drug related items at the same location."

"Harold, tell me were."

"Just a minute, let me finish."

"And, I have seen a man who has the four moles on his back, like you described."

"Who, is he, Harold? Who is he?

"Honey, I will tell you in a minute. Please let me finish."

"Okay. Please hurry!"

"Did you ever explore he idea that the HR part of the HR Baby comment the rapist makes could be for something other than human resources?"

"We could not think of anything else. Human resources sounded like such a good fit since most of the victims worked in that department."

"I heard someone say that, but it was in another context."

"Where did you hear it?"

"Let me tell you about everything I mentioned, including where I heard that comment.

"I saw the bottle in a locker at the ballpark. There was also a syringe and some bottle of some kind of liquid in the locker."

"You saw these items in a locker room?"

"Yes, at the ballpark. I also noticed one of my teammates had the four moles in the shape you described. I didn't notice it until we were talking about the rape victim's comments."

"What about the comment you heard?"

"I heard it after my teammate hit a home run. He said it after he had touched home plate, and sat down again on the bench in the clubhouse."

"What did he say Harold? Tell me, please."

"He said 'Home run Baby!"

"Why did he say that?"

"Because he was proud of himself."

"He sounds like he might be the rapist."

"He does have many of the characteristics, and the traits you have told me about."

"Is he a big or small guy?"

"He was a big guy."

"Harold, who is it?"

"It is Jing Heng."

"Do you really think he is the rapist?"

"He may very well be the guy."

"What should we do?"

"I think that tomorrow, you should coordinate your notes and facts, and then contact the police to set a time you can show them your evidence."

"But, what about all of the rapes in the other towns outside of Beijing."

"You mentioned the towns of Sichuan, Tianjin, Guangdong, Jianjin, Shanghai, and Beijing. You need to check Jing Heng's whereabouts on the dates of the rapes in those towns."

"How will I know that?"

"Go back the number of years that the rapist you are looking for was active in those towns. Then, get the baseball schedule for the Tigers in those same years and see if the team played in those cities on the dates in question."

"That is a good idea. I can check it on my work computer tomorrow."

"Akemi, please be careful. Turn everything you find out over to the police and let them handle the rest of the investigation. Will you promise me you will do that?"

"Yes, I promise."

"Thank you."

"Thank you, Harold. Come here, I want to reward you."

Chapter 23

A Tangled Web

April 26

AFTER HER INTERESTING discussion with Harold the night before, Akemi was up early the next morning, as she wanted to review what she had heard in regards to the potential identification of the serial rapist who had been terrorizing China for years.

She wanted to outline her work day, making sure she would find out all of Jing Heng's possible connections to the crimes.

First, she would list the dates of the rapes, and relevant information the victims might have revealed in their testimony about the attacker.

Second, she would categorize all of that data into a second list which referred to the attacker's characteristics or mannerisms.

Examples of these categories would be clothing worn, if "Big Hitter" cologne was smelled during the attack, the four moles on the rapist's back, the methods used in the rape, the attacker's possible personal use of drugs during the rapes, the drugs which were administered to the victims, and if the rapist used the phrase "HR Baby" during the attack.

Lastly, she would list the dates the Beijing Tigers had played baseball games, and their locations, and then cross reference that information with the dates and locations of the rapes, keeping in mind that all of the rapes had started shortly after midnight the calendar day after a ballgame.

Once the list was coordinated, Akemi would make a copy for her office, her home, and the police. She would then contact the Beijing police and make an appointment to talk with them about her data, and a possible suspect.

After kissing Harold goodbye, Akemi had headed to her office, and plowed into her tasks with great enthusiasm.

She loved being an unofficial detective, and looked forward to helping the authorities catch the man who had been terrorizing women in China for several years.

The task took several hours of intense research and review of the findings.

As she had expected, the data analysis showed a pattern. One hundred percent of the Rape Center's reported cases being investigated had taken place in the appropriate cities on the calendar day after a Beijing Tigers baseball game.

Akemi then needed to verify if Jing Heng had been with the team at home, and on road trips, the days of the rapes, which could be obtained by the police during the investigation.

After she had completed her report, Akemi had printed out three copies of the results.

She had then leaned back in her chair, and decided she needed a break from the intensive research and analysis task she had just completed.

Akemi had grabbed her Harold Gatewood autographed Beijing Tiger drinking mug, headed to the nearby employee lounge, fixed herself a cup of green tea with lemon, and walked outside to let the April sunshine warm her beautiful face.

Her office assistant, Janice Anderson, an American citizen working in Beijing, had noticed the furious pace with which Akemi had been working, and knew the topic of her supervisor's efforts were those of importance.

Sensing an opportunity to ease her curiosity, she had walked to Akemi's desk, read the title of the report, and recognized an opportunity to pass this information on to someone of great importance who would pay to obtain it.

Janice had quickly gone to the copy machine, made two copies of the document, and had returned to Akemi's desk, and placed the original report on her supervisor's desk, her actions all unseen by anyone.

The facts that Akemi's father was now President of China, and that his arch rival, Min Jun, was now vice-president had been the topic of political headlines in the Beijing newspapers for days.

Being a bright, ambitious woman, with a touch of larceny in her heart, Janice had laughed at the irony of the word larceny and its' derivative use of the name for W.C. Fields' main character in the 1939 movie, "You Can't Cheat an Honest Man", Larson E. Whipsnade.

She had also known that Vice President Min Jun would like to embarrass President Guo Gang, Akemi's father, in any way possible to have him removed from office, which would pave his path to the presidency.

Janice knew Min would love to get his hands on this information. She smelled a payday.

After Akemi had left for her lunch break, and a short walk before returning to work, Janice had gone outside, called the office of Min Jun, and had spoken to his chief of staff.

"Hello, I would like to speak with Vice-President Jun."

"What is your name, please?"

"Janice Anderson."

"Ms. Anderson, what is the nature of your call?"

"I would like to speak with the Vice President on a matter which will be of interest to him."

"Is this a political, or a personal, matter?"

"It is political in nature."

"I will connect you with Mr. Jun's staff member."

"Thank you"

"Hello, this is the Vice President Min's staff member, how can I help you?"

"Hi. I have information that I think will be beneficial to Mr. Jun."

"We get these types of call often. What are you calling about?"

"It is a sensitive matter, political in nature, and one which can be very beneficial to his political career."

"I need more facts than that."

"It can perhaps help him reach the presidency."

"Please give me more information."

"Take my word for it, this may be very useful for him."

"What does it concern?"

"It is sensitive data and information that would cause a scandal if it goes public."

"I am not sure you have anything in which Mr. Jun would be interested."

"Would you be willing to take a look at the information if I came to your office?"

"I will talk to you if you will come in, but you will have to promise you will not waste my time with trivial matters, or our conversation will be very brief."

"I promise you that he will be interested in the information. Can I see you late this afternoon?"

"Yes, I will be here all day."

"I will be in around four, thirty."

"Okay"

Janice Anderson had told Akemi that she had a dental appointment, and that she had to leave work early in the afternoon. She then headed to the meeting with the vice-president's chief of staff.

Secured in her purse was the information about the rapes, the victims, and the ties to the suspect.

After she had presented the detailed information to the vice president's chief of staff, she had waited for his positive response, and then stated that she wanted to be compensated for delivering the report, as she wanted the vice-president to ascend to the throne, and oust Guo Gang.

When asked why she felt so strongly about the matter, she said that she disliked the president, his policies, and his family, especially his daughter.

She had been insistent that the report was valuable, and demanded five, hundred, dollars for the information.

The Chief of Staff had looked at Janice, pondered his possible actions, then reached in his upper, left, hand, desk drawer and had withdrawn five hundred dollars in Chinese currency, and handed it to Janice.

"Obviously, Ms. Anderson, this is a serious matter, one which demands confidentiality."

"I understand. I will keep our meeting today a secret."

"Excellent thought Ms. Anderson. If you have any more relevant information on this matter, please call me again."

"I will."

Once Janice Anderson had left his office, the chief of staff knocked on Vice- President Jun's door, and asked to enter.

'Sir, I have some information which I believe may be beneficial for your career."

"Please let me see it."

"It discusses the serial rapist about which the public is concerned."

"This is interesting. How much did it cost us?'

"Five hundred dollars."

"It was a steal at that price. Good work."

"Perhaps we can take credit for the arrest of the suspect. That would increase your popularity with the public, sir."

"True. But I have another use for this information."

"What do you want me to do?"

"Contact this suspect, and tell him we can make this go away if he will perform certain services for us."

"I'll arrange a meeting with the suspect, and one of our operatives."

"Yes, do it now."

"Is there anything else I should do?"

"No. I will make a call to the head of the police department and handle matters with him."

"Very well."

"After his assistant had left his office, Min Jun made a call to the head of the Beijing police department, Tu Zan, to put his plan into action.

"Tu, this is Min."

"Hello Min. "What can I do for you?"

"I have information, and a situation, from which we both can benefit."

"What does it concern Min?"

"It concerns the serial rapist."

"Do you have a suspect Min?"

"Yes."

"Do you want me to arrest him?"

"No, I want you to hold off. Let's meet tonight."

"Okay. Come to my house for dinner. We can talk afterward."

"I will bring a report with me. Someone you have an appointment with tomorrow will also bring you this report and press you to arrest the suspect."

"The woman from the Rape Center?"

"Yes, Akemi Gatewood, Guo Gang's daughter."

"She is to arrive at ten o'clock tomorrow morning."

"I want you to follow my plan, as it will have better outcomes for both of us, and it will help me gain the office of the presidency. Then, I will name you the leading police and security officer in China."

"I understand."

"I will see you at your home this evening."

Chapter 24

"We want to talk with you"

April 28

AKEMI HAD GATHERED her report on the rapes, and the profile of the rapist, and had met with the head of the Beijing police department, Tu Zan, the day following Janice Anderson's visit to Vice-President Min Jun's Chief of Staff's office.

Mrs. Gatewood had high expectations for the capture and arrest of the suspect the research had pinpointed for the crimes.

Upon returning to the office after her visit to the police station, her disappointment was very noticeable to her office co-workers by the obvious dejected look on her face.

Her conversation with Mr. Zan had turned out to be a dead end, as the police department had not seen the evidence in the same light as she had.

In their opinion, there were too many rapes which took place on the days in which the Beijing Tigers had played their games. Their thinking was that not all of the rapes could have been carried out by the main suspect.

Much of the evidence was based on statements or opinions of people who had passed away, or had left the area, and could not be found.

The police also rejected the accuracy of the two eye witness accounts, as they were considered unreliable since the victim had been drugged, and was still in a state of confusion when they supposedly heard the suspect's HR Baby vocal statements.

Akemi felt like crying, but called Harold instead, telling him the outcome of her meeting with Mr. Zan.

Harold suggested that she relax, and realize that it would take time for the authorities to develop more clues and information, based on Akemi's report, which would serve as the cornerstone for the police investigation.

After Harold's encouragement, she was able to settle down, and concentrate on her other work duties at the rape center.

Jing Heng had been relaxing in his penthouse apartment, when he answered a phone call from a man who claimed to be with the office of the vice-president of China.

The caller was blunt, and to the point, in his initial comments to the Tiger first baseman. "Mr. Heng, we know that you are the rapist. We want to talk with you."

After a long silence, Jing Heng finally answered, "What are you talking about?"

"We have two witnesses who have identified you as their rapist."

"That is nonsense."

"We know your baseball games dates align with rapes in the towns where you played with the Tigers."

"So, what?"

"We also know that you say to yourself, HR Baby, after you hit a homerun."

"What does that have to do with anything?"

"Two witnesses have identified you as the man who said that when he was raping them."

"They are lying."

"We also know about the cologne called Big Hitter."

"What does that have to do with anything?"

"We also know about the four moles you have on your back."

"It is not against the law to have moles on your back."

"We are going to have you arrested tomorrow morning if you do not agree to meet with us tonight."

"I doubt it."

"We have connections, and can make this go away, eliminating the jail time you will have to serve if you don't cooperate with us."

"How can you do that?"

"We can do what we want. We are at the highest levels of power in the government."

"So. what?"

"So, you are soon headed for arrest, trial, conviction, and prison. my friend."

"I will never serve a day in prison."

"In that respect, you are correct."

"What do you mean?"

"Because we are going to kill you if you do not cooperate."

"You can't do that."

"Yes, we can. And, we will, kill you soon, maybe tonight or tomorrow if you don't cooperate.

"I don't know who you are but this is ceasing to be funny."

"To prove to you that we are not fooling around, put down your phone, walk to your front door, open it, and pick up the envelope which is laying on the rug in the hallway. It contains the addresses of the last two women you have raped. Both live in Beijing."

"Quit bothering me."

"Do it, or there will be an immediate reprisal by the gunman across the street. We can have him place his sights on you, and you will see the red dot on your chest slightly above your heart."

"Come on. Don't be ridiculous."

"Okay, since we must prove it to you, I am ordering my assassin to sight in on you, and let you see the red target dot on your chest."

"Stop it."

As soon as Jing Heng had finished speaking, a red dot appeared on his chest, slightly above his heart. Shaken, he answered the caller.

"You could just be shining a lazer at my chest."

"Go to your front door, and pick up the envelope in the hallway."

"Alright, I will humor you. Then, you need to leave me alone."

Heng went to his front door, opened it, saw the envelope on the hallway floor, stooped down, and picked it up.

He then turned, headed back inside the apartment, opening the envelope as he walked. After he had opened the envelope he stopped walking, his face turned red, and he became silent.

"Mr. Heng, what did you find?"

"I found the envelope."

"What do you think of the two addresses?"

"I don't want to answer you."

"Of course not. But, are they accurate?"

"Maybe I should see you."

"Yes, I think that you should. We are across the street, and we will be right up, Mr. Heng."

After a knock on his door, the ballplayer had looked through the peephole, and had then opened the door.

Two Chinese men, one even larger than Heng, walked inside, each brandishing a pistol at their side.

One of the men had then motioned for Jing Heng to sit on the couch. He then followed their directions, and made himself as comfortable as he could, under the trying circumstances.

"Do you now believe that we are with the government?"

"Yes."

"We know you are the rapist."

"I would still get my day in court."

"Where you would be convicted, if you were able to live that long, which you would not be able to accomplish, as we would kill you first."

"How can I get out of this situation?"

"You have only one option. You must do as we say, in every aspect."

"What do you want me to do?"

"You are not enthralled with one of your teammates."

"Yes, Harold Gatewood. I can't stand him."

"Mr. Heng, we know you are using performance enhancing drugs."

"How do you know that?"

"We have watched you use them in this apartment."

"I have not."

"Shut up! Do you think we are stupid?"

"No."

"They are in your bedroom, in the box on the shelf in your master bedroom closet."

"How did you find that out?"

"We have been watching you."

"What must I do to Harold Gatewood? Kill him?"

"No. If we wanted him dead, he would have been eliminated long ago. We want you to do a little mission for us at the ballpark tomorrow."

"Okay."

"Yes, once it is done, then you will tell the press that you thought he had been a problem as soon as he joined the team."

"Why must I tell the press after he has been caught?'

"Because you are a Chinese hero, a homerun king, and your comments will help smear Gatewood's reputation."

"Is that all you want me to do?"

"Yes, that is all for now."

"Will you ask me to do other things in the future?"

"We will let you off the hook when we decide it is the right time to do so."

"I do not mind helping smear Gatewood. In fact, I would enjoy that action. But I do want some sign of assurance and good faith that you will not hurt me, or my career, later."

"As long as you do what we ask you will be fine. If you cross us, or fail to do as we order, we will kill you immediately."

"I will do what you ask."

"Congratulations, Mr. Heng, you are not as dumb as you look."

Chapter 25

"What's that?"

April 29

THE CLUBHOUSE HAD been quiet as the Beijing Tigers dressed, and prepared for the game against the Henan Elephants, who would be in town for a four-game series.

The usual laughter and banter that accompanied the card games was absent, as were the music devices, which routinely blared its menu of Chinese ballads and love songs in a high pitch.

The Beijing Tigers had lost the game one to nothing the day before, managing only one scratch hit.

The Tigers had dropped their fifth game in a row, and were now five games out of first place, behind their arch rival Tianjin Leopards, who had swept the four-game series at the end of the recent road trip.

Change in direction was needed, everyone had hoped that it would take place with the current game with the Elephants.

The Tigers' hopes for change would materialize, but not in the manner they had expected.

Harold had usually been the first or second player to arrive at the ballpark each day. On this day, when he had entered the clubhouse, he was shocked to see Jing Heng sitting on a stool in front of his locker, as he was usually the last player to arrive each day.

Harold had said hello and asked Jing how he was doing today, to which the huge first baseman had grunted a response, one which resembled a gurgling sound, as if a person was drowning.

Gatewood put on his shorts with built in jock strap and cup, sliding pads, sanitary stocking socks, then added his stirrup baseball socks on top of them, then his lightweight long sleeve sweatshirt, then sat down and read his mail, which had been sent to the ballpark.

The usual batch of fan mail and autograph request letters were opened, read, and organized for responses, which were handled by a woman Akemi had found to handle her husband's ever- increasing mail volume.

Harold had continued to read his mail. He then smiled when he saw the return address in the upper left-hand corner of the envelope of one of the letters.

It was from Enrique Rodriguez, his driver in Havana, Cuba, who had squired him around when he was in the country scouting the World Baseball Games for professional baseball.

Harold continued to smile, often stopping to remember the events of over two years ago, when Enrique, in his beloved old car, the gold and white colored, 1959, four-door, hardtop, Sport Coupe, Plymouth Belvidere, had driven he and Christina Abene to many locations in Cuba.

As he sat in front of his locker, memories, good and bad, crept into his mind.

He remembered Enrique taking Christina and he to the beach for a romantic getaway, where he had given Christina the beautiful necklace, he had bought from his friend Spencer Robinson, the diamond broker, and how the ballplayer had escaped an assassination attempt by AIO assassin Bakar Kemen.

Harold also thought of the time Enrique had taken the couple to Pinar Del Rio for a weekend getaway, and to conduct his baseball clinic with the Cuban pitching prospects.

Sadly, he also had remembered Enrique dropping off Christina and he at the Havana airport for their flight back to America.

Horrifying memories of her assassination by ETA operative Bakar Kemen, and her dying in his arms at the airport brought tears to Harold's eyes.

He had remembered her final words, telling him that she loved him, and his act of picking up the necklace he had given her, which had fallen from her neck to the floor during the shooting.

Harold had also thought about Christina's wonderful qualities, and the other good memories of the Cuba trip, all of which eased his pain.

Enrique and his family were doing well. He had written to Harold to congratulate him on his wedding, and the fact that he was back in baseball.

Harold had put the letter in his locker, had planned to write Enrique soon to thank him for his letter, and to wish him well.

A surprise visit by the drug testing team for the China Gold Baseball League was conducted before the start of pregame workouts. Harold was one of the players who had been selected for testing, and had given his urine sample to be analyzed by the testing service's lab.

While returning to his locker, Harold had noticed that one member of the testing team had stopped at his locker, and had looked around, not touching anything, but Bakar just looking.

As Harold approached his locker, the inquisitive man said "What's that?", as he pointed to a small bottle of liquid on the top shelf of the locker.

Harold said he didn't know, picked up the bottle to look at it, and noticed the testing team member looking over his shoulder. Suddenly, the observer blurted out a series of sentences.

"Performance enhancing drugs Mr. Gatewood? Please explain why there are PED's in your locker!"

Harold was stunned but did manage to say that, whatever was in the bottles didn't belong to him, that he had no idea how the bottles had gotten into his locker, as he had never seen them before, and that he had never taken drugs in his life.

The clubhouse then broke out into mass confusion, with several of Harold's teammates coming over to his locker to see the bottles of the substance, and the three members of the testing service also coming over to view the bottles.

Accusations were hurled at Harold, some by his teammates, and some by the testing team, all of whom wanted answers.

Tiger's manager Hui Jun had also walked to Harold's locker, and had tried to restore order.

Harold had watched in silence as the ugly scene had escalated, and then resumed normalcy.

After he successfully calmed down the shouting group of players and testing members, Manager Jun asked Harold to come into his office, where they discussed how the drugs had gotten into Harold's locker, if he was on drugs, and if he knew anything at all about the situation.

Harold's answers were, that he had no idea how the drugs had gotten into his locker, that no, he was not now, or ever had been, on drugs, and that he had no idea what was going on in regards to the situation.

While Harold was in Manager Jun's office, Scott Binder had noticed Jing Heng laughing as he faced his locker, so as not to be seen by other people in the clubhouse.

Heng had laughed, giggled, and smiled during the entire ugly scene with the drug testing members.

In an attempt to quiet down the episode, Harold was ordered to sit out this day's game, until more details related to the event could be determined.

He was advised to go home, as the manager did not want him to have to face the press, and the circus atmosphere which was sure to break out one the news of the event was made public.

As Harold headed home, he was angry, and wanted to find out who had betrayed him, and set him up for the upcoming drug investigation.

On the walk to the apartment, Harold called Akemi to tell her what had happened, and that he had no idea what was going on in regards to his situation.

She had offered to come home from work, but Harold told her that she should stay at her office, as he needed time to settle down, get over his anger, and try to figure out what had happened.

The scene at the ballpark turned from one of shock, to disbelief, to pandemonium, to ridiculousness, to wild speculation, and to the conclusion that Harold was a doper who should be banned from Chinese baseball.

News of the event hit the radio airwaves even before game time, and would be the headlines of the newspapers the following morning, all of which made the situation much worse.

When Akemi came home after work, she walked toward Harold, put her arms around him, kissed him, told him she knew he was not involved in the dug situation, and that he was the honorable man she would always love.

The next morning, the newspaper headlines were merciless in painting Harold as a disgrace to the Tigers, the Chines Professional Baseball League, to the city of Beijing, and to the country of China, for his actions.

He was becoming the scapegoat for the Tigers losing streak, which had now reached six games, after a second loss to the Elephants on the day when the news of the PED's in Harold's locker had been found.

Jing Heng had conducted himself in a manner foreign to his usual surly self on the day drugs were found in Harold's locker. He had broken his personal rule of refusing to speak with the press, and had freely given interviews to any news or television outlet who had asked for one.

He had continued his criticism of Harold on the early morning media shows the day after the PED's were found.

Heng was proud of himself, and unknown to the public, was confident that he had put his personal problems in regards to the multiple rape situations behind him.

He now thought that he could return to his once-held, mantle as the face of Chinese baseball, an honor he had held for years, before Harold Gatewood had come to town.

He had celebrated Harold's dismal day by hitting a prodigious home run in the twelve to one loss to the Elephants, and by enjoying splendid evening of rape on another female Beijing resident, one who also worked in the Human Resource Department of a large manufacturer, and who had heard the phrase "HR Baby" at the precise time of his sexual release.

Vice President Min Jun was also proud of himself. His enforcers had convinced Jing Heng to cooperate in what would now become a continuing assault on Harold Gatewood.

That assault was designed to bring misery and disgrace to his rival, President Guo Gang, his wife Aiko Gang, the woman who had refused his marriage proposal, their daughter and Harold Gatewood's wife, Akemi Gang Gatewood.

Yes, Min Jun's plan to bring down President Gang, and his family, and to assure his rise to the Presidency of China was in motion, and looked like it would soon sweep him into office.

Chapter 26

Purgatory

May 6

IT HAD BEEN a week since the scandal about Harold's potential usage of PED's had burst forth into public view.

It had been a rough time for Harold, as the print and electronic media had been relentless in their attempts to find out any the details related to what type of scandal might exist.

Harold had been raked over the coals unjustly, and had been set up by someone who wanted to take him down.

The newspaper headlines had been brutal. Samples of the witch hunt were slanted toward a guilty man who had abused his attained position and talent, a man who needed to be brought down to size.

Harold had read the headlines the day after the PED's were found in his locker in the clubhouse.

Gatewood Tied to Drug Scandal

Is the President's Son-In-Law a Doper?

Is Tiger's Star Gatewood A Cheater?

Gatewood Denies PED's In His Locker Were His

Harold had vowed that he would not read any more newspapers, or watch television about the growing scandal. He had decided to center his thoughts on finding who had planted the drugs, and how he would expose them.

He had also released a statement for the media which stated his innocence, his pledge to find out the people behind the planting of the drugs, and his mission to clear his name and reputation.

He also vowed to stay in shape, and return to the workout program which had transformed him into the best physical shape of his life.

He did his daily Tai Chi and Taekwondo workouts, his interval running program consisting of walking then running predetermined distances, and a light weight lifting regime.

All of exercises helped slowly conquer his anger, aggression, and stress level which was eating away at him.

He had decided he would stay strong, and remain ready for his return to the Tigers, whenever that might take place.

Harold had adopted a schedule where he would arise early, have breakfast with Akemi before she went to work, do his workout, and then research some of his favorite hobbies in the afternoons prior to Akemi returning home.

Harold had learned that hunting in China was almost nonexistent for the main body of the population.

Chairman Mao had banned the sport in 1949, despite the presence of pheasant, rabbit, pigeons, Pere David deer, six species of red deer, Sika and Hog deer, tigers, snow and clouded leopards, wildcats, lynx, four species of elk, Sambar, goats, numerous varieties of mountain sheep, civet, alligators, wolves, and fox.

Harold had realized that if the sport was ever recognized by the Chinese upper levels of government, the new market for hunters would be a bonanza for businesses like his own, which booked hunting trips.

Fishing in China was allowed, and heavily practiced. Many canals had been dredged in the Beijing area in 2006, and offered bait and pole fishing for the masses.

Grass carp and the small, golden, colored Crucuian carp were the favorite catches of public, and often ended up on the supper plate. The practice of fishing with Cormorants was also practiced in China, as it was in Japan.

Other species of fish in the country which drew the attention of the public were Armur catfish, pike, and goby, Northern Pike, snakehead, sturgeon, and the many ocean species, including mullet, snapper, sea bass, Spanish mackerel, and cod.

As Harold had considered the list of available fishing options, he had decided he wanted to take a trip with Akemi to the Chinese area of Inner Mongolia to fish for the world's largest species of salmon, the taimen.

Harold had also researched the growing popularity of the sport of golf in China.

While the sport was usually too expensive for the general population to play, golf was very popular in the upper income groups of China.

Foreign investment had drawn foreign golf fanatics to come to the country to play the many great courses and to watch the many professional tournaments.

The China Golf Association sponsored the Volvo China Open, and the Grand China LPGA tournament was sponsored for the ladies' professional players.

The BMW Asian Open, the TLC Classic on Hainan Island, and the Pine Valley Beijing Open were other professional tournaments which drew world-wide notice to China's love of the sport of golf. Harold had considered taking

Akemi to a tournament once they could escape the nightmare of the PED scandal.

Akemi had supported Harold through the difficult week with her love, and her ability to listen to his worries and his plan to comeback after the scandal was placed in the past.

They had played pool, worked with the weights, and swam in the apartment complex recreation area.

They had taken walks, discussed their life plans, and made love endlessly during the week.

Harold's parents had called twice, offering their support, and assuring them that the scandal was manufactured, and Harold would be soon playing ball again with the Tigers after he was vindicated.

Akemi's parents had also offered their support, and told him not to listen to, or worry about, the smear tactics which had tried to tie the scandal to the Presidency, saying it was just politics which would soon flitter away.

The Beijing Tigers had continued their downhill slide, extending their losing streak to eleven games.

Scott Binder had called, telling Harold that he had spoken to management about the manufactured scandal, and the need to reinstate him as soon as possible.

He had also mentioned that manager Hui Jun was on the hot seat, and had been called on the carpet by upper management that he must turn the team around or be fired.

Scott also mentioned that all of Harold's teammates, except one, had signed a pledge of support for his return to the Tigers. Only Jing Heng had refused to sign the support pledge.

Scott had expressed disgust that, while everyone else was feeling down, Heng was on top of the world, as he had hit four homeruns since the day of the scandal.

After Scott's call, Harold had asked if there had been any reported rapes in Beijing since the day of his suspension.

Akemi had mentioned that there had been four cases, the dates of which meshed with Heng's rape history.

She had also interviewed the four victims, and had heard many of the same aspects of Heng's rape procedure, including the "HR Baby" comment.

The couple had talked about the need to continue to build a case against Heng, and that the new information should be turned over to the head of the Beijing police.

While both were disgusted with the slow pace at which the police were progressing in the investigation, they had agreed that it would unfold at the pace at which it was destined, and that the police would do what they needed to close the rapes and build a legal case against Heng.

Harold's workout for the day had started in the usual manner, and he had now found himself in the small park near his home in which he did his workout.

The park was a half, block, sized, area, with the unusual characteristic that it was complete with green grass, and contained a small area with slides, swings, and imitation animal s upon which the children could sit and rock back and forth.

While it was not the world's greatest park, as far as parks go, at least it was usually deserted, as it was today, or sparsely visited, during the mornings.

Harold completed his stretching and meditating exercises, and his running program, then sat down on a swing, to glide back and forth like he had done as a little boy in the North Park, near the Little League diamond and across the blocked off street from the swimming pool, in Gibson City.

As he had gained height on each succeeding glide of the swing, he thought about all of the events which had taken place in his life, and why he had now found himself in this position.

He was just a ballplayer, playing the game he loved.

His career and reputation, built up over many years of hard work, had died the day of his suspension, and was now mired in its own version of purgatory, waiting to be resurrected. He would make that happen, no matter what he must do.

He had had the park to himself, and had accomplished his mission for the morning, when he noticed a tall figure, dark complexion, hair, moustache, and eyes, walking in his direction.

As the man moved closer, Harold noticed that the man looked to be of a decent which could be found in Miami or Dallas, in America.

The man carried something in one hand, which made Harold think the approaching figure was right-handed.

The closer the man became, the more Harold was able to learn about his face, which was marked by a chiseled jawline, shining brown eyes, white teeth, and a small half-moon, shaped, scar on his cheek.

The man stopped short of the swing, and said hello, to which Harold responded in kind.

While Harold was cautious, the conversation continued. When Harold had asked where the man was from, an answer was given that he was from Spain, and that he had gone to college in Madrid.

The man's conversational tone was pleasant, relaxed, and unforced.

He had said that he was in China on a business trip, and had read about the events which had led to Harold's presence on the swing.

He had also said that he felt Gatewood was being crucified by the media, and that he would soon receive his special kind of justice.

Harold was unsure of the man's purpose for their conversation, but continued to talk with the stranger.

The more the man talked about his world travels, his refined speaking manner, his unique problem-solving business skills, his love of the finer things in life, and his love of playing cards, mainly poker and baccarat, the more Harold realized the person in front of him was a Renaissance man.

"If I can ask you, you mentioned that you have special problem-solving skills. Can you tell me what they are?"

"I use a strong, swift, and deadly approach for my opponents to solve unique problems, and to administer the special type of justice that my victim deserves."

"Your victims? Do you mean your business opponents?"

"No, I mean victims, which is what you will soon become Mr. Gatewood."

"What are you talking about?"

"I am going to administer my problem-solving skills to remove you this earth for creating and continuing to be a problem for the AIO, and for killing my two cousins, Bakar and Bittor Kemen."

All of the man's intentions were now on the table, and Harold, who has suspected as much, had tried to keep the man talking, which would give him time to plan his response.

As the man had taken his hand from his right jacket pocket, and removed a small pistol, Harold had almost giggled at the weapon, as it resembled a small toy gun.

At the same time Harold had dropped from the swing to the ground, narrowly dodging the two rounds the assailant had fired.

While on the ground Harold rolled to his right and delivered a leg sweep with his right leg to the man's knees, knocking him to the ground, and causing him to accidently flip the pistol to the right of his previous standing position.

Both men jumped to their feet at the same time, and assumed fighting positions.

A barrage of Taekwondo jabs, hand thrusts, kicks, and blocks were unleashed by both angry possessed, participants of the brawl.

The action continued unabated until the aggressor landed a round house kick to Harold's left cheek, rattling his teeth, causing him to see stars, and then drop to the ground.

Without missing a heartbeat, the AIO operative was on top of him, his hands wrapped around Harold's throat.

As the man's large hands compressed tighter and tighter on the victim's windpipe, Harold felt the life draining from his body.

He felt like he was going under, on his way to what he had always believed would be a better place.

As Harold continued to lose strength, and feel as though he never again see Akemi, or the children they had hope to have, he became increasingly more helpless.

Harold then noticed the aggressor's face, complete with the hatred in his eyes, the snarl on his mouth, and the determination to kill him in his eyes.

After what he thought had been a car backfire, the victim then watched the assailant 's eyes glaze over, his mouth droop, his grip on Harold's throat relax, and his body slump down on the ground to the left of Harold's pone body.

Still stunned and gasping for the breath of life, Harold gathered his wits, and eventually sat up.

He wondered what had happened, as his attacker was now dead, shot through the back of the head by an unknown guardian angel of the American baseball player.

Afraid of what might happen next, Harold walked away from the park, and back to his apartment, knowing that, once again, he was lucky to be alive.

Harold reported the attack to the Beijing police, who picked him up at this apartment, and returned to the park to process the crime scene, and take Harold's statement about the events in the park.

Once Harold had been questioned, the police escorted him back to his apartment, where he called Akemi to tell her what had happened, and that he was feeling alright.

In the office of the head of the Beijing police department, the man in charge of the investigation called the Vice-President of China, Min Jun, with the news of the attack.

Min was elated about the news, and made sure to order the police chief that he should call the media immediately and provide the details of the attack and murder.

The next morning's paper contained the headline "Gatewood Attacked and Involved in A Murder in A Beijing Park".

The lengthy article covered the mysterious shooting of a citizen of an address near Vitoria, Spain, a Mr. Eneko Itzal, and an entire rehash of the Harold's PED scandal.

Min Jun could not believe his good fortune. He was enjoying the fact that his plan to smear Guo Gang had received such an unexpected bonus, with attack on Gatewood.

The event could now be spun in the media in a direction which would attempt to tie Gatewood in possible AIO terrorist events in China.

Min was gloating, and looked forward to presenting Gatewood with more hurdles, and horrors, related to his desired innocence in the PED scandal.

Everything was falling into place, and soon, Gatewood, and Guo Gang, would be no longer be standing in his path to the presidency of China.

Chapter 27

The Tiger Lives

May 20

THE ROOM WAS silent, as eight men, patriots at heart, had said their helloes, then had taken their appropriate seats at a large rectangular-shaped table.

On the wall above the chair at the far end of the table was the red, green and white flag of the Basque people, a flag which the eight men felt as though they had failed.

A tall, black-haired, mustachioed, man rose from his chair and spoke, his voice, usually booming and confident, was reduced to a whimper, as he dreaded to announce the bad news to his comrades.

"Welcome fellow freedom fighters. Long Live the Basque people."

"Welcome! We salute you."

"Scribe, please note the presence of the three Regional Commanders, their Assistant Regional Commanders, the Assistant National Commander, and, myself, Ekain Koldo, the National Commander."

"Completed, sir."

"With our attended members, all three areas of our AIO organization are represented. Those areas are our Logistics, Political, and Military divisions."

Nods of the eight heads acknowledged each of the division representatives.

"Tonight, we continue our long struggle for self-determination, establishment of our country borders, the free use of our language, and the enjoyment of our proud culture.

May we always be free, never again to suffer the indignities forced upon us by the dictator Franco."

Seven pairs of hands pounded the table in half-hearted approval of the National Commander's comments, as they knew from the expression on his face that the news they would soon hear was probably not good.

"Our meeting tonight will dispense with the usual reports, as you have emailed them to me, and which I have copied and placed in front of you on the table."

"We see them, sir."

"Gentleman, tonight our meeting will address one topic. The bad news is that the Tiger lives. Operation Tiger Slayer has failed."

"How did I happen?"

"Our operative, Eneko Itzal, was adept in mapping out a successful attack plan, and had the target in his grip, in the process of causing death by asphyxiation.

"What went wrong?"

"He had nearly eliminated the target when he was shot through the back of the head by an unknown assassin."

"By whom?"

"We have no confirmation of that yet, but we have our usual list of suspects."

"Sir, what are we going to do now?"

"That is why we are here tonight, Gentleman. What are your thoughts?"

"Sir, I think that our mission is compromised due to our weak presence in China."

"I agree. We have no organizational backup, and we continue to lose our best operatives because of this action against the specific target."

"Sir, we all agree that we want to eliminate the target at any cost. but we need to step back and analyze how we can now accomplish that task, without any more failures, and losses of our agents."

"Yes, I agree. Sir, perhaps we should wait until the target is located in an area more conducive to our success."

The discussion went back and forth, with members discussing the pros and cons of continuing the mission to eliminate their nemesis.

A vote was finally taken, and Operation Tiger Slayer was halted, for the time being.

In another area of the world, another meeting was also taking place in regards to the failed attempt on Harold Gatewood's life.

CIO Director Rick Owens was at his desk, reviewing reports and details about the capture of another American naval vessel which had been captured in the Persian Gulf, when his right-hand man Deputy Director Terry Robbins knocked on his door and asked if he could come in, as he had some news.

"Come in Terry."

"Thank you."

"I know you are monitoring the capture of the American naval ship by the Iranians."

"Yes, the Iranians are continuing their aggression in the Persian Gulf."

"Yes, this is yet another incident with our navy."

"This one will probably be rectified on a basis which does not include death, or follow up military actions."

"Yes, but it does get old. They continue to push the envelope."

"I am afraid there will be more incidents in the future."

"Sir, I have new information on Harold Gatewood, and his situation in China."

"What is it now?"

"As we discussed, he survived the assassination attempt by the ETA agent Eneko Itzal. Now, he has been cleared to play baseball again."

"Good for him. How will that affect our agent's mission in China?"

"He will again be playing games in Beijing, and on the road in various cities. Our agent will now need to follow him while he is on the road also."

"The AIO will probably try again. And, there are other people still wanting to even the score with Gatewood."

"The Yakuza is one of them."

"What is the status of the situation between President Gang and Vice President Jun?"

"It is still very strained. The experiment to place Jun in the vice presidency has not been working, as the old issues are still strong. Some people think the situation is worse than before."

"And, of course, there is Gatewood, in the middle of the spat."

"Correct."

"Very good Terry. Please alert our agent Jack Taylor and our man in the American Embassy, Roger Caldwell, of the plan."

"I will, do so."

It had been two weeks since the AIO had tried to kill Harold, and it had been three weeks since he was suspended by the Tigers.

The good news was that Harold had been cleared in the investigation concerning his supposed usage of PED's, which were found in his locker.

He was exonerated because no direct evidence existed to prove Harold had placed the drugs in his locker.

His past history, and the fact that he had asked to clear his name by taking a drug test every day, which had been shortened to three times a week, also helped prove Harold's innocence.

Today would be the first game Harold would play, as he had finally become antsy being at home, and was nervous about how the fans would react to his presence in the lineup against the Shanghai Golden Eagles.

In his first at bat, Harold was fooled and hit a weak ground ball to second for an easy out. His second at bat was another weak ground ball to the shortstop. His third at bat was no better, as he hit a dribbler back to the pitcher.

The Tigers had won the game, one to nothing, on a home run by Jing Heng.

As he watched Heng circle the bases Harold wondered what events might take place in the early hours of the following day.

Heng did not follow his usual habit of refusing to talk with the beat reporters who covered the Tigers, but talked at length about his home run, and how he planned to lead the Tigers back into contention for the division crown.

When asked if he was glad to have Harold back in the lineup, Heng had ignored the question and continued to talk about his game winning hit.

Heng was heading to the showers as Harold was finishing drying off his hair, and preparing to leave. He noticed a paper which had fallen to the floor from Heng's locker, and when no one was watching, he walked to Heng's locker and picked up the paper.

He read it carefully, then read it again to make sure he had read what he had thought he had seen the first time.

Harold then placed the note on the top shelf of Heng's locker and started to walk home.

Once outside the stadium, and out of listening distance from anyone on the street, Harold called Akemi on his cell phone.

"Hi."

"Hi. How did the game go today?"

"I am glad to be back. My timing was off today."

"How were the fans?"

"They were wonderful. They clapped and yelled loudly."

"Were all of the yells complimentary?"

"Stop teasing me. Almost all of the yells were those of encouragement. But here were a few catcalls."

"Catcalls. My parents must have been at the game."

"Ha! Ha! Good one, my dear. I am so sorry that I have unintentionally caused your parents some grief."

"They understand, and they love you."

"Akemi, please listen closely. I have something very important to tell you."

When Harold had finished. Akemi answered him.

"I understand. I will do that right now."

Jen Heng had been in a joyous mood after his heroics of Gatewood's first day back in the lineup. He had won the game with his home run, and had managed to steal the spotlight from the American's return to the Tigers.

He had decided that he deserved a very special reward for his day's efforts. For his evening meal, he chose his favorite dish, Peking Duck, at his favorite restaurant.

When Heng dined out, he usually sat in his usual secluded, dark corner of his favorite restaurant, spoke with no one, not even his server, as he would hand a written note to him, or her, with specific instructions on his order, and how his meal should be served, his water and beverages should be refilled, and every aspect of how he should be treated.

Tonight, it would be different, as he was outgoing, signed autographs, and was gracious to his servers, and everyone he encountered.

He was celebrating in anticipation of his well-deserved, special treat.

It was just before midnight when she had turned off her bedroom lights in anticipation of a sound sleep, one in which she would not have to get up the next day until she wanted to, as it would be the weekend, and she would have two days of freedom from the grind of work.

The large man, in black, ninja-like, clothing, waited for a few moments to give his intended victim time to go to sleep, and to allow the excitement of the coming attack and rape to build inside his mind.

This one would be a glorious event, his best of the many, he had committed in many cities in China.

He had performed the ritual since he was a teenager in the poverty-stricken area of the country.

The rapist had reached the pinnacle of his craft, and was the true ultimate professional, a king of the act, in his own eyes.

He had looked in both directions to make sure that there was no traffic on the side street which bordered the back of the apartment building.

Once the coast was clear, he had walked across the street to the back door of the building, taken out his lock pick, turned the door, and entered the back hallway.

He had placed tape over the door latch which slid into the door jam, in order to keep the door from completely closing, in case he needed to make a quick getaway if events turned bad.

Slowly, he had walked up the back stairs to the apartment where his chosen victim, his favorite, and the one which had given him the most pleasure in the many rapes he had performed over the years, was now sleeping.

He relished the thought of surprising her, cupping his hand over her mouth to prevent her from screaming, and to experience the thrill of gaining control over her, and seeing her shudder in terror of what he might do next.

Silently, he also dreamed of his act of binding her hands together, then to the headboard of the bed, so she could not resist, and of also binding her ankles to each corner of the bottom of the bed, spread eagle, so she could not kick him in his vital areas, or prevent what he had planned for her.

He hoped he would not have to strike her in her beautifully, shaped face, as he did not want to leave any bruises.

He had looked forward to seeing her wonderful dark brown eyes as he performed the act.

The large, dangerous, man had wanted to feel, and stroke, her gorgeous dark hair as he pleasured himself, as the touch of it had aroused him immensely during his first attack.

He had fantasized about her many times since their first travel to the pleasure palace together, and tonight he had planned to let both of them enjoy the experience again.

In his lifetime, he had not married, had children, or even fallen in love with a woman, but tonight, he had planned on being with the woman who had stolen his heart, even in the perverse manner he had come to know her on an intimate basis.

He loved her, but did not know why.

Maybe it was because she had made him feel relaxed during the act, and that she had seemed to care for him, even when the attack had finished, and she had laid sobbing on the bed.

For some unknown reason, he had stayed with her for hours in an attempt to comfort her, after she had sobbed and broken down.

The rapist had grown close to her, especially when she had draped her right arm over his back when he had cut the bindings which held her hands against the headboard.

He did not know if she had done it as an unconscious act, or if she was somehow thanking him for staying with her on the bed, after the ordeal had ended.

It did not matter in either case, as he had grown to love her, in a perverse way.

The first time he had threatened her, saying he would harm of kill her if she did not surrender to his demands.

He had always regretted that action, and would not do it again this evening.

Once he had picked the door lock, and gained entry inside the apartment, he had quietly crept down the narrow hallway, opened her bedroom door, and walked toward her bed.

He had stooped to look at her long legs, both of which were draped over the outside edges of the blanket on the bed.

Her eyes were closed, and she had a smile on her face, as she lay sleeping. He had lowered his knife to his side and relaxed, enjoying his opportunity to continue admiring her, in all of her peaceful beauty.

Suddenly, and without warning, the beautiful girl had sat up in bed, and Bang! Bang!, Bang!, Bang!, Bang!, Bang!, six. Loud. shots had poured out of the four-inch barrel of her handgun.

Each shot struck the aggressor in the chest, rocking him back with each round that entered his body. His arms flailed they tore into his body.

He then crashed to the bedroom floor, and didn't move, as he was already starting his departure from the earth.

When the shooter had arisen from her bed, she smiled, knowing that the prone, now pathetic figure on the floor would never again terrorize her.

She had stopped three feet from her attacker, and had sworn at him for taking her dignity and pride away from her during, and after, the first rape.

The massive figure had then groaned, and moved slightly, and had then uttered the last words he would ever speak on earth, "Shu Yun, why did you shoot me? I love you."

The words had stunned Shu Yun, but once she had regained her composure, she reached into the pocket of her nightgown, grabbed and reloaded six more rounds into her .38, then said the last words her attacker would ever hear.

"Well, I don't love you, HR Baby!"

Then, she had proceeded to fire six more rounds into the victim, three more in the chest, and three in the man's crotch.

Chapter 28

Boomerang

May 21

AFTER COMPOSING HERSELF, and as Jing Heng lay dead on her bedroom floor, Shu Yun called the police to tell them that a rapist had entered her apartment, and that she had shot him dead.

When she had finished giving the police her address, she sat down on her bed to relax.

She couldn't help but look at the monster who had raped her, and had crept into her bedroom with the intention of doing it again. She had waited for this opportunity, and mercifully, it had arrived.

After a knock on her front door, and an announcement that two uniformed police officials were in the hallway, she walked to the peephole, spied a man and a woman in full uniform.

She then insisted that the officers show their badges. She then opened the door, let them come inside.

With firearms drawn, the police officers searched the apartment. After a call was placed for a forensic team and an ambulance to come to the residence, the officers took Shu Yun's statement concerning the identity of the victim and the details of the shooting.

The intended rape victim was then taken to police headquarters from an official statement.

She was made comfortable in an interrogation room, given a cup of tea to drink, and told to relax.

The identity of the victim was well known, and when it was learned by the police, they had contacted the police chief, who had gotten out of bed and come to the police station to personally speak with the victim.

Before leaving his home, the police chief had made a phone call to Vice-President Min Jun, who was awakened and forced to leave the pleasures of a sound sleep by the call.

Once the identity of victim was discussed, the two men plotted a strategy to be followed.

When the shooter entered the interrogation room, the police chief was struck by the beauty of the woman who had killed Jing Heng.

Despite her harrowing experience, she still possessed the classic, Fibonacci, ratio-shaped face, and beautiful features, all of which might be hiding a cold-blooded killer.

A taped conversation of the events of the evening then took place.

"Please give me your name."

"Shu Yun."

"Please give us your account of what happened in your apartment this morning."

"A man entered my apartment to rape me."

"How did you know he was a rapist."

"He had done it before, and was coming back to do it again."

"Please tell us the how the events unfolded."

"I went to bed, shortly before midnight, and did not go to sleep, as I knew he might be breaking into the apartment shortly."

"How did you know that?"

"I was told by my friend who works in the rape center."

"Who was that?"

My friend is Akemi Gatewood."

"How did she know the man was arriving that night, and planned to rape you?'

"Her husband told her."

"Who is her husband?"

"Harold Gatewood."

"The baseball player?"

"Yes."

"How did he know the man would be breaking into your apartment?"

"Akemi said that he figured it out at the ballpark."

"Okay, tell us what happened inside the apartment."

"I waited in bed with my pistol, pretending to be asleep."

"Did you hear him enter your apartment?"

"Yes, I heard him turn the lock, slide open the safety chain, enter the front room, and creep down the hallway."

"Were you afraid?"

"Yes."

"Why didn't you call the police in the first place?"

"Because I had a weapon to protect myself, and I wanted to kill him for what he did to me the first time.

Akemi told me that I should be ready if he tried to attack me again, and that the pistol would protect me, and eliminate my problem once and for all."

"What happened after the man entered your bedroom?"

"He took his tools out of his rape kit."

"What do you mean by his tools?"

"A syringe, a date rape drug, and a cord to tie my hands and feet to the headboard and the bottom of the bed."

"Then what happened?"

"He started to walk toward me, then I sat up in bed and shot him six times in the chest to kill him."

"Then what happened?"

"I walked from the bed, and shot him six more times."

"Was he already dead when you walked toward him?"

"No."

"Did he say anything to you?"

"Yes."

"What did he say?"

"He asked why I shot him, and he said he loved me. I then told him that I did not love him."

"Then what did you do?"

"I shot him six more times to make sure he was dead, and to make sure he would not hurt me, or any other woman, ever again."

"Where did you shoot him?"

"The first six shots, from the bed, went into his chest. The next three, when I was beside him, also went into his chest, and the last three went into his groin area."

"Why the groin area?"

"Because that is what he used to hurt me the first time."

"Is there anything else you want to say?"

"I am glad he is dead. He will not rape another woman again. And, I am glad the Gatewood's warned me of his plans. They saved my life."

"Do you have a safe place to stay tonight?"

"Yes, I can go back to my apartment."

"Are you sure?"

"Yes."

"We are done processing the crime scene so if that is where you want to go, we will take you home."

"Thank you."

"Don't leave town. We may want to talk with you again."

"I won't."

After the investigation, the Vice President Min Jun was called to inform him of the full details of the young lady's comments.

The vice-president and the police chief discussed strategy, and outlined the steps to be taken in order to gain full benefit of the situation.

The vice-president had complimented the police officer on how he had handled the matter, and promised he would be handsomely rewarded for his assistance.

The newspaper headlines that morning were blockbusters, ones which did Harold and Akemi no good.

They were painted as the masterminds behind the shooting, and killing of the male victim. Harold and Akemi could not believe what they were reading in the papers.

"Akemi Gatewood, Daughter Of The President, Advised Rape Victim To Shoot Her Attacker"

"President's Daughter Urges Killing"

"Gatewood Urged Killing Of His Teammate"

Harold and Akemi's treatment in regards to their good deed was also disgraceful on the morning television ad news programs, and on the radio talk shows.

Their actions to help Shu Yun had boomeranged on them in a most devastating and ugly way.

Akemi was distraught, and after calling in sick at her workplace, cried her way through the morning.

Harold was angry, and had split his time between supporting Akemi and denying the rumors on each of the phone calls he received from members of the media.

The country was abuzz with the situation, with some people criticizing the Gatewood's actions, and some people praising them as heroes who had helped stop a serial rapist. The anti-gun lobby in the country also weighed in on the matter, declaring it as a senseless act of violence could have been prevented if the police had been contacted.

The president, Akemi's father Guo Gang, was roundly criticized by his political opponents for his daughter and son-in-law's actions, which they had called disgusting, and supportive of a gun and violence culture, which was out of line in respect to the country's views of citizen's possession of firearms.

In the United States, CIO Director Rick Owens and Deputy Director Terry Robbins were once again troubled by Harold Gatewood's role in another scandal, and had contacted Roger Caldwell at the American Embassy in Beijing about the matter.

Fearing another attempt on Harold's life, they had also instructed their field operative Jack Taylor, to continue his assignment of monitoring the ballplayer's movements, and his safety.

In Tokyo, Japan, Yakuza Yamaguchi Gumi crime family head Masaru Hayato had sensed an opportunity for his assassin, Isamu Goro, one which would allow him to eliminate Gatewood during this tumultuous and stressful time for the American, as his concentration and alertness would be distracted.

In Madrid, Spain, the AIO National Committee, now on the sidelines in the Harold Gatewood assassination lottery, hoped that another person or organization would do what they had failed to do, kill their nemesis.

As the Vice-President of China, Min Jun, sat at his table on the patio of his residence, in the Beijing sunshine, reading the headlines of the morning's newspapers, a smile spread from one end of his face to the other in gleefulness.

"Things are working out better than I had planned. Mr. Heng and his connection to me in the PED scandal was eliminated by the actions of the young woman whom the president's daughter urged to get, and use, a gun."

He smiled again, and continued his thoughts.

"And, Harold Gatewood himself has been tied to the scandal. I would like to see Guo Gang's face this morning, as he is now embroiled in another loss of face situation."

Then, Min Jun, broke out in hilarious laughter. He then said, "This is going better than I had hoped. I will now institute the next step of the process."

Chapter 29

Innocent

September 15

AFTER HAROLD HAD arranged for Yong Wei to take Akemi to her parents' residence for company and safety, Harold had left the apartment to walk to the Tigers' ballpark.

At the entrance to the stadium, he was greeted by a crowd holding signs, some of which were supportive, and some of which were not.

The crowd was split in equal numbers, some hailing Harold as a women's rights hero, and some as a villain who had been responsible for the killing of their beloved "Home Run Heng".

Harold had stood in a confused state, unable to process what was actually in front of his eyes, when a beautiful Chinese woman named Bai Haun, whose name meant Pure and Happy, of which she resembled neither, bolted from the crowd, ran to him, threw her arms around him, and kissed him long, and passionately, on his lips.

She then yelled an odd, rambling, untruthful series of sentences.

"Harold, I love you, and I know that you had nothing to do with the murder. We have talked many times about how Heng was a disgrace to the Tigers. I will always be here for you."

Finally able to free himself from her grasp, and her crazed speech, Harold then waded through the crowd, through the front gate into the stadium, and down the stairs to the safety of the clubhouse.

He told Scott Binder about the incident in front of the stadium with the crazed woman. Unknown to Harold, the kiss had been captured by the series of press and paparazzi photographers outside the stadium.

Harold had then been called into the Tigers' front office to explain his side of the newspaper headlines.

Harold explained what had happened, and what he had seen Heng do over the course of the season.

Harold also told management that the case against Heng for a series of rapes had been turned over to the Beijing police, and that there were so many damming facts and connections to the rapes that he would have soon been indicted.

He mentioned that dates, times, and locations of the rapes corresponded with his known movements.

Upper management had sat in stunned silence, and had finally agreed to support Harold, and let the ugly incident pass.

They also had mentioned that while they were satisfied with his play, the amount of outside publicity was distracting to the team, and that they had considered releasing him from his contract.

Harold had one reply.

"I am just a ballplayer. All of these events are not my, or my wife's, doing. The truth will come out, and both of us will be vindicated for all of the things that have happened to us in China."

The next day, the saying that things sometimes go from bad to worse, was in full display in the newspapers and the voice media, as pictures and videos of Bai Haun kissing Harold in front of the ballpark were shown and seen on every media outlet.

The newspaper headlines were true to form.

"Gatewood's Mistress Supports Him at The Tigers Stadium"

"Beautiful Mistress Pledges Support for Gatewood"

"Gatewood's Mistress Kisses And Tells"

"Gatewood And Mistress Publicly Dispute His Role In Killing His Teammate And Rival" Harold and Akemi had been through many rough times in their short time together, but nothing was as destructive as the current incident.

Akemi didn't believe that Harold had been unfaithful, but was devastated by the attack and shameful implications spoken and published about her husband.

Harold was angered by the wickedness of the media, and had told Akemi that they needed to find a safer haven in which to live and prosper.

Only their love for each other mattered and the truth would prove both of them innocent of all the horrible lies and accusations that had been heaped upon them.

Shu Yun was not faring much better either, as she had been arrested for the murder of her rapist, Jing Heng.

She had been slated for indictment, and trial, as soon as possible.

It would become a televised, country-wide circus when the case came to trial.

The country was split along the typical lines of thought which were in play when a woman murders a man during a supposed rape attempt.

It would be bruising court battle. Hers was not the only murder of interest in the trial, as Janice Anderson was mysteriously murdered before she could testify about her knowledge of the first rape Heng had committed on Shu Yun.

As the weeks dragged on, the trial, and Harold's alleged affair with Bai Huan, stayed as a topic of focus for the media outlets.

It was China's version of the worst picture of the court system. Mercifully for Shu Yun, she was found innocent of Heng's murder, thanks in large part to the information Akemi had found out about his locations and actions.

He had been proven to be involved in a long series of rapes in multiple Chinese cities, and was classified as a deceased serial rapist.

Akemi's records of Heng's first rape of Shu Yun were also instrumental in her innocence.

Several additional witnesses had come forward to identify him as their rapist, and confirm his rape procedure, including the "HR Baby" comments. At last, Shu Yun was free.

While all of the eyes of China had been on Harold and Akemi, three sets of eyes in particular were focused on Harold, for quite different reasons than his alleged involvement in the Heng murder trial.

Yakuza hitman Isamu Goro had been tailing Harold for months, hoping for the right moment to eliminate him, without drawing unwanted notice to the crime family.

To this point in time, he had been stymied, as his target was seldom alone, due to the flock of press who tailed his every move away from the ballpark.

Another set of eyes belonged to Jack Taylor, who on his protection mission for Harold, had encountered the same ever, present, pack of media jackals who followed Gatewood's every move, and complicated the CIO agent's task in many ways.

It was frustrating work, but Taylor was dedicated to his mission, and had developed a sense of respect for Gatewood, and his courage to survive the numerous situations which had threatened his life over the last four years.

A lesser man than Harold Gatewood would have chosen the easy route, discarding his stated goal.

The third set of eyes belonged to Masaru Hayato, head of the Yamaguchi Gumi crime family in Tokyo, who wanted revenge for Harold's role in his parents, and sister's deaths, and the humiliation of his crime family, and the Yakuza organization names.

Masaru had been closely watching the events in China, and was eager for Gatewood's demise.

Despite the outside interferences, Harold had played very well, and the Tigers had crept back into the division race.

They had started their resurgence thirteen games out of first place in May, and had narrowed the gap to two games off the lead as the team had rolled into Tiajin for the final three games of the year, a road series with the Lions.

The first game went to the Tigers by a score of three to two, highlighted by a game ending catch in left-center-field by the Tigers outfielder, with the Lions having three men on base.

The second game was a pitching battle, with the Tigers prevailing in a one to nothing victory. The division race was now tied, and would be decided tomorrow.

As the Tigers boarded the bus which would take them back to the hotel, Harold was the last in line, as he had spoken to a reporter for a brief moment about his expectations for the final game of the season.

As Harold waved goodbye to the reporter, and started to enter the bus, a man behind tree located across the street, sighted in his rifle, and aimed at his target, a man hiding in the bushes to the right of the Tigers' team bus.

He adjusted his scope to clearly see the man's face, which was now set in a look of determination.

The man with the rifle stood motionless, watching his target, prepared to pull the trigger of his rifle at the precise moment which would end the life of his intended victim.

As Harold turned to enter the bus the shooter pulled the trigger, and a speeding cartridge started its flight through the air, centered on the middle of the victim's head.

A loud pop was heard, which to Harold Gatewood sounded like a balloon bursting.

The cartridge sped forward, passing through the target's head, causing him to slump, then fall, dead before he hit the ground.

The target lay dead amid bushes that surrounded him, as Harold Gatewood and his Tiger teammates started the journey to their hotel.

The dead man, a Japanese assassin for the Yamaguchi Gumi Yakuza crime family named Isamu Goro, who had followed the ballplayer for months, had failed in his mission to terminate Harold Gatewood.

He had fallen prey to CIO agent Jack Taylor's cartridge, which had passed through Isamu's head and into the trunk of a small tree behind him.

Agent Taylor had then slowly broken down his weapon, placed it in its case, walked slowly to his car, then headed to his hotel, the same one in which the Tigers were staying.

For today, his job was done.

Chapter 30

"Mission Accomplished"

September 16

THE SEASON HAD BEEN a long one, and it had all come down to the last day, with the Tigers and the Lions tied for the division crown going into the last game.

Harold had sat at the breakfast table in the hotel and thought about the events which had brought him to this point.

He had endured the highs and lows which were becoming typical in his life, some of which he hoped he had seen the last of.

He had also become happily married, had made another what he hoped would be a successful step in his comeback, had played very well, and was looking forward to today's game for the bragging rights of the division.

He hoped it would be his last game as a Beijing Tiger, as he wanted to take Akemi to America, and play in the major leagues once again.

Harold had also suffered many horrifying events, including his near death by strangulation by the AIO assassin Eneko Itzal, a second assassination attempt by Yakuza hitman Isamu Goro, a phony PED scandal involvement, a suspension from his team, a false accusation that he had been involved in the murder plot of the worst person he had ever had as a teammate, Jing Heng, and had been accused in the media of having an affair with a woman he had only met one time.

The false reporting of the Bai Haun affair had gone on for months.

The woman had staged the phony kissing episode for the press at the ballpark, had continued to go to home games and cheering for her "Honey", Harold Gatewood, going to road games and getting a room in the same hotel where he had stayed, calling him constantly and leaving messages, and telling the press repeatedly that she was having an affair with him.

Harold could not determine if she was mentally ill, or was being used by someone to create scandalous publicity to damage his reputation, for an unknown party.

Gatewood had not positively identified the man behind the scheme, but after several conversations with his father-in-law, President Guo gang, he was certain it was Vice- President Min Jun who was the mastermind.

Harold had finally taken out restraining orders against Bai Haun which prevented her from coming within fifty yards of Akemi or himself, and outlawing any contact with the couple.

The situation was still present, but had dwindled down to her making herself seen to the couple from distances over fifty yards, and in which she would not speak or motion to the either Harold or Akemi.

As the scandal neared the end of its life, Bai died a mysterious death. It was ruled death by personal drug overdose. Harold had still believed that the vice-president was behind the woman's death, made in an attempt to silence his role in the scandal, but he could not prove it.

He and Akemi had been through a lot this season, and they were ready to go on a nice, relaxing trip as soon as the baseball commitments were finished for this season.

They had talked about several options, and had whittled down the list to two.

In an attempt to keep family peace, as Akemi and he expressed different choices for their vacation destination,

Harold had suggested that they go on both trips, with a two- or three-week break sandwiched in between.

The vote for the suggestion was an enthusiastic yes from both parties.

The final game would place Scott Binder on the mound for the Tigers, against a battered pitching staff of the Lions, who had been cursed with many injuries all year.

The Lions had squandered a thirteen, game, lead, and were now in a sudden, death battle for the title.

The top two pitchers in their rotation had gone down with injuries, and had already undergone Tommy John surgery with Doctor Doug Washington in America, the same surgeon who had saved Harold's career.

The rest of the Lions pitching staff had struggled, and were overworked. The starter for the Lions was a fastball, curveball pitcher, one whom Harold had hit well this season.

If he were to depart the game for any reason the Lions would use their starter from the first game of the series, on short rest, to takeover.

He was a two-seam fastball pitcher, with a cutter, and a changeup. Harold had struggled against him in the series first game, and during the year.

From that point, the Lions would use their regular bullpen, overworked that it was, with setup men for the seventh and eighth inning, and their regular closer, one of the best in the league, in the ninth.

Harold would be catching again, as his body had held up, and his arm had remained sound. He had caught over ninety games, despite being suspended for three weeks for the false PED scandal, and had returned to his former self in the field.

He knew he could catch again, and would have caught well over one hundred games had his season not been interrupted due to false scandal.

He knew that the scouts who had watched him catch this season were also of the same opinion.

The day was a beautiful one on which to settle what team, the Tigers or the Lions, would move on to the next step in quest of the Championship.

The game started off with an explosion as the Tigers, prompted by Harold's grand, slam, home run, scored six times in the first inning.

Scott Binder was then rocked for five runs in the bottom of the first, and it looked like the bat boys of both teams would be pitching the ninth inning if the trend continued.

The Tigers were held scoreless for three innings while the Lions added two runs in the second to take the lead, two more in the third, and one in the fourth innings.

The Tigers had five more innings to erase a ten, to, six deficit, and everyone on the team knew they could do it, as the Lions pitching was struggling, giving up hard hit balls for outs.

The Tigers had stranded two runners on base in the second and third innings, and three in the fourth, making a total of seven men left on base, a very disappointing occurrence.

In the fifth, Harold led off with a solo home run, which accounted for the only run for the Tigers.

In the bottom of the inning the Lions added one more run, making the score eleven to seven. The seventh inning for the Tigers was a productive one, with three runs scored on six hits.

The bottom of the seventh, and the eighth inning, were scoreless, with a resulting eleven to ten lead for the Lions.

In the top of the ninth inning, Harold hit screaming line drive home run to right center field off a sinker from the Lions ace closer to tie the score at eleven runs apiece.

The Tigers then went down in order, and took the filed in the bottom of the ninth inning.

The Tigers had exhausted all of their pitchers except one, a tall, right-handed pitcher with a sinker, medium grade two seam fastball, and a slow breaking curve ball which served as his changeup.

The Lions leadoff hitter was the one hitter the Tigers did not want to see, as he had been terrorizing the Tigers all day.

At breakfast in the hotel restaurant that morning Harold had seen where the hitter and his wife had been blessed with the birth of their first baby, a boy, named after the father.

Harold looked forward to the day when Akemi and he would have children. And he was happy for the Lions player, but hoped he would stop his rampage against the Tiger pitchers.

When the tall, lanky Tiger pitcher took Harold's sign for a sinker, he shook his head, signifying he wanted to throw another pitch.

Harold then signaled for a slow curve ball on the outside corner to the left-handed hitter.

Again, the Tiger pitcher shook off Harold's signal. Harold did not want his pitcher to throw a fastball unless it was outside and away from the hitter, and signaled for the slider once again.

The pitcher stepped back off the mound, took his cap off, and ran his fingers though his long hair.

Harold had walked toward the pitcher's mound to remind the pitcher that fastballs needed to be kept away from this left-handed hitter, as he was a terrific fastball hitter. The Tiger pitcher said he would do so, after which Harold headed back to the plate.

Despite his better judgement Harold called for the pitcher's medium grade fastball, hoping it would be kept on the outside part of the plate. As soon as the ball was delivered, Harold thought "Oh, oh", this is not going to be good.

In what was the hitter's wish for his newborn son, a pitch was coming to the plate wrapped on a bow for a left-handed, power hitter who liked a pitch low and inside.

Harold watched the hitter's bat come through the plate and send the ball skyward like a rocket headed for outer space.

It went, and went, and went, for what seemed like an eternity, landing over five hundred feet from the plate.

Harold thought that the new father's home run would not come down before his new baby had graduated from college, but it mercifully did.

The Lions erupted in joy, rushed the field, and welcomed their hero to the plate.

Despite all the excitement, Harold tried to make sure the hitter actually touched home plate, as his dad had always taught him.

The welcoming committee grouped around home plate made Harold's task impossible, and as the hitter jumped into the air and landed somewhere in the vicinity of plate, they rushed to congratulate their hero.

The Lions were division champs, and the Tigers' long season had ended. Harold always hated to lose, but deep down, he was glad this season was over.

In Beijing, news of the Tigers' loss was a disappointment, but it was secretly appreciated by some, one of which was Vice-President Min Jun, whose name meant clever ruler.

Jun hated the Gangs and the Gatewood's so much that he was rooting for the Lions. He laughed at his ability to keep this fact secret, especially from Guo Gang.

Shortly after the game ended, Min Jun received a phone call from President Gang, which requested that he come up to the observation deck on the top of the governmental office building.

Gang wanted negotiate a peace treaty about their differences, and have a drink to seal a pact of agreement between them, as they both watched the sun go down over Beijing.

Min agreed and made his way to the top of the building, where the two rivals began to talk.

"Good evening, Min."

"Hello, Guo. Thank you for coming up here."

"You're welcome."

"Min, we have always had our differences, as we have discussed many times before."

"I know, Guo."

"Is there any way we can come to a truce, for the benefit of the people of the country?"

"Yes, there is a way."

"What is that, Min?"

"You could resign, Guo."

"So could you Min. That is why I asked you up here."

"I will not."

"Then I am going to ask the Communist Party leaders to demand it."

"You do not have the votes, or the power, to get that accomplished, Guo."

"I will when I tell them about the evidence I have that details your actions."

"What details?"

"I know you have subverted the legal system in the Shu Yun murder trial, to prevent your use of the Jing Heng in the PED case against my son-in-law from becoming known to the public."

"You can't prove that, as Heng is dead, and I ordered the drug overdose death of the only other witness with damaging testimony, Janice Anderson."

"I have proof of that also."

"How?"

"She kept a record of the payments you made to her."

"I think you are bluffing."

"I am not."

"You were never a good poker player, Guo."

"Min, Bai Huan has confessed to receiving your payments, and that you had her claim she and Gatewood had an affair, in an attempt to discredit him, my daughter, and my family."

"She was cray, and she was hooked on cocaine. No one will believe her."

"She wrote down the payment details, Min."

"I don't think so."

"You have two choices, Min. You can resign, or you can jump to your death,"

"I will do neither."

"Then I will ruin you, Min."

"No, you won't. Get your hands up, Guo. As you can see, I now hold a gun on you. I offer you the same two options, resign, or I will force you to jump.

If you do neither, I will shoot you. and then say you became irrational because your administration is failing, and tried to kill me because you blamed me for your failure."

"Min, that will not work, as I have already given the evidence to the party leaders."

"Then I have nothing to lose, and am going to shoot you. My only regret is that Aiko and Akemi are not here to see you die."

"I am here, Min."

A voice behind Min Jun had alerted him to the fact that there were now three people on the rooftop.

"Aiko, I am glad you are here to watch your husband die."

"I do not think so, Min."

"Why, are you going to stop me?"

"Yes."

"I don' think so."

With that definitive comment, Min Jun turned, faced Guo Gang, cocked the hammer on his weapon, and started to squeeze the trigger.

A loud bag erupted from behind the vice-president, and a bullet from a revolver held by the president's wife tore through Min Jun's back, exiting trough his heart, and out the front left side of his chest. He was dead before he hit the rooftop.

Aiko Gang had finally settled the decades old feud between her husband, and Min Jun. Guo Gang walked to his wife, took the weapon out of her hand, and put his arms around her.

No words were needed, as what had needed to be done for decades, was now accomplished.

Chapter 31

Taimen

September 28

THE NEWS OF Vice President Min Jun's death was announced the morning after his shooting.

After the proof of Min's guilt in his political actions against President Guo Gang, including the attempts to implicate Harold and Akemi Gatewood in false incidents and scandal-laced rumors, and the video tape of the events on top of the governmental office buildings were released, the evidence vindicated Aiko Gang from murder-related charges.

Min Jun had used the unlawful actions of a serial rapist, Jing Heng, in the false connection of Harold Gatewood to a performance enhancing drug scandal, and he had used the false accusations of a deranged woman, Bai Huan, in a claim of an ongoing affair with the ballplayer.

Harold and Akemi were vindicated and all tint of scandal was removed from their names. Major League Baseball also renamed Harold as an official supporter of their development centers in the country.

The loving couple had celebrated the good news with a quiet evening at home together, topped off by a tender night of lovemaking.

As the couple had lad in bed after making love, and telling each other how much they were committed to one another, Akemi told Harold that she wanted to tell him something very important.

"Harold, you know that I love you."

"Akemi, I love you too."

"The next apartment we get needs to have two bedrooms."

"To have room for an office so you can work at home?"

"No."

"Why would we need two bedrooms?"

"We need two bedrooms because three people need two rooms."

"Akemi it's just you and I."

"Not any more Harold. I am pregnant."

"You are? Wonderful! This is so great. How many weeks?"

"Sixteen weeks. The baby will be born in late February?"

"Akemi, I am so happy!"

"So, am I."

"I can't wait to tell our parents."

"We will tell them tomorrow."

The cries of joy from Gibson City, Illinois were almost audible in Beijing, as Harold's parents were so excited. The same degree of excitement was present in the residence of the President of China, as Akemi's parents were also overjoyed with the news.

Both sets of the soon-to-be, new grandparents went immediately into baby shower planning mode, and would have all plans made by the time Akemi was closer to her due date.

It was a relaxed, joyous time for everyone, and a welcome break from the stressful summer they had all endured.

Akemi's choice of a fall vacation location was the protectorate and autonomous region on the border of China and Russia called Inner Mongolia.

They would fly to the capital city of Hohhot, also called Huhehaote, for a week of relaxation, lovemaking, and fishing for Siberian taimen, historically called the "The River God's Daughter", by the Han Chinese, the ethnic majority of Inner Mongolia.

The couple would travel one-hundred-fifty-miles upstream from the capital to their base camp, then fish for the largest of all salmons.

The trip included a guide and a cook, yurts stationed by the river in which to sleep, and beautiful scenery, which looked much like Montana in the American West.

Taimen were a beautifully colored fish, with an olive-green head, a brownish and green body, a white to dark gray underbelly, and dark red fins. It was a magnificent throwback to centuries ago when these giants were more numerous.

The Hucho taimen still survived in the wild areas of Mongolia and Russia, and were massive specimens of up to ninety-two pounds, six feet in length, and almost sixty years of age."

Harold and Akemi could expect to catch trophy fish in the thirty to sixty pound, forty-eight-inch range, which would test of their equipment, and their skill. In addition to the taimen, the couple could expect to catch Armur Pike, and grayling.

It would be a glorious adventure, set in a beautiful setting, where the couple would fish within a few feet of their yurt, make love by the stream, and enjoy a week wonderful together.

It was to be a perfect escape from the rigors and stress of the Tigers baseball season.

The fishing results were outstanding for both Harold and Akemi, as the couple caught many fish in the thirty, pound, and up, range, scores of Armur pike up to twenty pounds, and more grayling than were needed to fill the frying pan each evening.

Akemi was to take top honors for the largest taimen, with a forty-eight-pound, six-ounce, monster, while Harold's best came in at just over forty pounds.

Each evening the couple would watch the beautiful star-filled sky after supper, then retire to each other's arms in the yurt for the night.

Their guide was a local man who had lived on the river his entire life, and had learned the river's bends, depressions, and depths from his father.

He was a quiet, gentle man, one who belonged on the river, and who had little interest in anything else.

Their cook was the opposite, talkative to the point of aggravation for his listeners, full of outlandish stories, and cursed with forgetfulness.

The employees of the outfitter were the odd couple in terms of makeup.

On the third day of the trip, the cook realized that he had forgotten to pack most of the trip's special dietary needs for the pregnant wife, and the ballplayer who was almost a vegan in terms of eating habits.

The dust of the dirt road kicked up a swirl that reminded Harold of the tornadoes he watched in Gibson City, Illinois, a swirling, upward-pulling, currents of air, powerful and dangerous in nature.

Soon, the cook and the camp vehicle, a survivor of past military Chinese operations painted in olive drab green color, had pushed up the dirt road, over the hill, and out of sight.

The guide, Harold, and Akemi fished from the bank, walking further and further from camp as the day progressed.

The guide knew where the deep holes were in the river, and had placed the campsite within walking distance from the yurts in order to accommodate any clients who were elderly and could not walk very far.

When those deep holes had been fished, the guide's procedure was to take the clients upstream in the military vehicle to a series of new spots to fish.

Harold's parents had mailed him a large rat-looking lure, nine inches in length, with single hooks, on which Harold's dad had filed down the barb points to make the lure barbless, which would protect the ancient fish the couple would be catching.

Harold would use a bait casting rod and reel to hurl the heavy lure into the river, and to use the oversized Husky Eppinger, red and white daredevil, lure to fish for large Armur pike.

Fly rods and reels were also used to fish with large mouse imitation flies for taimen and Armur pike.

Grayling were caught with many of the typical flies used in Canada and Alaska, black ants, olive winged doves, bug imitations, and almost any other black, colored fly that could be cast to the dimples on the water of rising fish.

A large taimen had broken off Akemi's mouse fly, the last of the supply the couple had brought to the steam on the day the cook had headed into town for supplies.

The guide offered to walk back to the supply yurt to pick up another refill of mouse flies, which Harold had agreed with instantly, as it gave him a chance to talk with Akemi about something he wanted to say.

"Akemi, I love you very much."

"I love you too, Harold."

"I'm so happy you are pregnant and that we are going to have a baby."

"So, am I."

"I forgot to ask you something very important."

"What was it?"

"Is the baby going to be a boy or a girl?"

"It is going to be a boy."

"Wonderful."

"Yes. We will go for a girl next time."

"What should we name him?"

"Maybe, Tai."

"Tai?"

"Yes, short for taimen."

Harold burst out laughing, and was quickly joined by Akemi. After a couple minutes of giggling and talking about the baby being a boy, the couple started to again cast into the slowly moving current of the river.

The guide had made his journey back to his yurt, and was now thinking about how many mouse flies he should bring back with him to the river.

As he opened the door of the yurt, a flash of steel headed toward the man's abdomen, finding home and burrowing in four inches in depth into the guide's flesh, and tissue.

The only sounds in the yurt were the impact of the entry wound, the "uh" sound of the victim when the knife blade had entered his body, the sliding sound of the blade when it was removed from the abdomen, the thud of the victim's body when it fell forward and came to rest, and the slow, dripping sound of the blood droplets as they hit, then splattered on the floor.

It had been a quick, surprise attack that had dispatched the victim quickly and silently, and which had now freed up the attacker to make his move on his real reasons for being in Inner Mongolia, all down by the river.

The aggressor then peeked out of the yurt doorway to plot his approach, and crept toward the riverbank, using bushes and foliage for cover.

Soon, he was within ten feet of the couple, still undetected. Akemi had hooked, and played a large taimen, thirty-one pounds in weight, to the shoreline.

Harold had moved streamside to lead the large fish to the bank, to remove the hook, then hand it to the woman who had hooked and successfully played the fish to the shore, for a picture. As he turned to accomplish that mission, Harold saw the flashing steel of the long blade of the knife, dropped the fish, and moved toward Akemi to protect her from an attack.

Gatewood's instincts were correct, but he had been too far from Akemi to prevent the attacker from swiftly moving to her, and grabbing her around her neck with his left arm, while holding the knife in his right hand.

"Now, Gatewood, you will do as I say."

"What do you want?"

"I want to kill your wife, and then you."

"Why?"

"You both caused the death of my sister, and later, of my father and mother."

"We did not cause any of those actions."

"Oh, yes you did. If you had not come from America to play baseball in Japan, then none of this would have taken place."

"That is ridiculous. The events you described were caused by their own actions."

"I disagree, and it is too late, Gatewood."

Harold rushed toward the man, but he slipped on the wet riverbank, and fell on his knees.

By the time he reached the attacker, Akemi had been stabbed three times in her abdomen, and her throat had been cut. Harold had seen Akemi's eyes as she looked at him as her throat was being cut.

Gatewood had screamed to stop the attack, but he could not cover the distance between them quick enough.

He had then crashed headlong into the attacker, causing both of them to fall to the ground, and causing the knife, now coated with Akemi's blood, to fly through the air, and land in the dirt and mud on the ground.

Harold and the attacker rolled and wrestled on the ground, trading punches, insults, kicks and bites.

Both men had death on their minds, and in their hearts, and the battel ragged on until Harold was able to slug his opponent with a viscous right hand which knocked out the killer's two front teeth.

Harold was now sitting on top of the man, pounding him with blows to the face, until he suddenly grabbed the man's throat and started to grip it tighter and tighter, as the man tried to free himself from Harold's choke hold.

As Harold gripped the man's throat, he felt rage and hatred for his assailant, who now deserved all the punishment Harold was dishing out.

The ballplayer saw the life start to disappear from the man's eyes, and increased his choking action with all of his strength.

The man's resistance grew weaker and weaker. Harold knew what the man was thinking, as he had experienced it himself when Eneko Itzal had tried to strangle him in the park in Beijing.

The stages of death that Harold had experienced, were now taking the man he was choking, as he experienced shortness of breath, panic, struggling actions to free himself from the death grip, and an advancing movement toward his passing out, then into his journey into death's dark tunnel.

The killing of Akemi, and his unborn soon, fueled Harold's continuing choking action, even though he knew the man was now dead.

He could not stop himself, as their deaths were now his driving force for revenge.

Soon, other thoughts entered his mind.

He was angry about the events of the last four years, his banishment from major league baseball in America, the losses of Lore and Christina, and all of the pain he had endured.

He knew the man was dead, but he kept choking him for ten minutes, trying to right all of the wrongs that had been heaped upon him.

Gatewood then threw the man's lifeless body to the ground, where it landed in the river, and stayed next to the bank.

The current then started to gain control of the corpse, plotting to move it into the main channel, and downstream.

Soon, the river won out, gently taking the body into the current, down the center of the river, and around the bend, never to be seen again.

It would become protein for the bears, or the wolves which lived in this region of the country.

Harold had not felt guilt, shame, or disgust for what he had done. He had avenged Akemi and their unborn son's deaths, and he had made sure that the man, Yakuza Yamaguchi Gumi crime lord Masaru Hayato, would not terrorize anyone else ever again.

He then walked to Akemi, sat down, and pulled her body onto his lap. He held her tightly, her blood staining his clothes, and put his right hand on her abdomen, where their now dead, unborn, son still resided.

He sat in silence for hours until the camp cook had returned with the supplies, the absence of which had caused his departure earlier in the day.

The cook had walked to the riverbank, and had asked Harold if he was alright.

Harold did not answer, but continued to sit, devoid of feelings of humanity and hope, which had now been drained from his mind and body.

His eyes were fixed on the river current, moving downstream, and around the bend.

Harold wondered where life's current would now take him.

Truthfully, he did not care much in what direction that path might be.

Printed by Libri Plureos GmbH in Hamburg, Germany